# LAKESIDES AND LONGING

## A MICHIGAN MILLIONAIRES ROMANCE

### KIMMY LOTH

Copyright © 2022 by Kimmy Loth

All rights reserved.

No part of this book may be reproduced in any form or by any electronic or mechanical means, including information storage and retrieval systems, without written permission from the author, except for the use of brief quotations in a book review.

# CHAPTER 1

Blake stood out on the deck of the ferry and let the breeze ruffle his hair. He loved this ride even though it was on the chilly side. It was peaceful, though not terribly effective at erasing the memory of the last twenty-four hours.

He was surprised he'd even made it here.

He had been between jobs and decided to give the love of his life one more shot. Debbie had left him three times—the last right before he planned to propose—but he couldn't let her go.

Well, at least not until he showed up in Kyoto and found out she wasn't there on a business trip, but a honeymoon. He was such a fool. He'd really thought she'd just been scared of commitment, not him, but then she went and married the Italian playboy she'd run off with.

He was gutted and numb. Love wasn't something he understood. All he knew was that Debbie took his heart and smashed it to pieces. He'd never love anyone again, and he had to give himself time to grieve and heal.

He wanted to find a job that would distract him. As a pharmaceutical research scientist, he never had a steady job, only projects. He didn't need it. Several years ago, he'd created a medication that helped lessen the side effects of chemo and made a fortune. He'd never have to work another day in his life if he didn't want to, but he did like his work, so he did projects. He was involved with a few top-secret projects with various governments and so even if he didn't seek work out, it came to him at least once a year.

What he needed right now was a good trek in the jungle to find a poisonous spider or snake that would cure a rare disease. But none of his contacts panned out.

So he got on a plane and flew back to the States. He spent a few nights with his buddy Tristan in Florida and then hopped into a rental and drove north with his Doberman, Tria, not stopping until he reached Michigan.

Why Mackinac Island, he didn't know.

But it was as good a place as any to clear his head and mourn his loss. And his buddies, Lukas and Hayden, would see him through it.

Tess set a cup of coffee down in front of him. She'd welcomed Blake into hers and Lukas's home, no questions asked. Lukas had definitely found a keeper.

"Sorry if I woke you guys up," Blake said. He'd taken the first ferry of the morning over. Hadn't even called to say he was there.

"No, Jack was already up. We just weren't dressed yet. I'm sorry about Debbie." She gave him a pained smile.

He shrugged. He'd spilled the whole story to the both of them the second he stepped over the threshold. They seemed happy to see him, and Dio was over the moon that Tria came to play. He hadn't seen his dog since he arrived. They were playing hard in the backyard.

"You think I can stay in the carriage house for the summer? I just need to be somewhere I can recharge for a few months. I'm between jobs, and I just don't want to think about her. You know, even after Debbie left me in Prague, I figured we'd get back together at some point." It'd been a few years, and he'd talked to her a couple of times.

Thank goodness for best friends. Blake had no living family. Lukas and Hayden were the closest things to brothers he had, and they lived three doors down from one another. Truthfully, he thought about going to Hayden first because his wife Anna had become Blake's best friend in the whole world, but he knew they were not morning people. He'd visit them this afternoon.

"Yeah, sure. No problem. I'll call Estelle and get it cleaned up."

Lukas's cell buzzed. He picked it up and stepped out of the room, leaving Blake with Tess.

"When are you due?" Blake pointed to Tess's swollen stomach.

She placed a hand on it. "September. Jack is getting a little brother."

They chatted a bit about Jack and the coming baby, and then Lukas stomped into the room, his face red like the inside of a watermelon. He clenched his fists, his jaw tight. It was a look that Blake had not seen on him often.

"What's the matter?" Tess asked, tensing. Apparently neither had Tess.

"It's Paige." Lukas had talked about his sister before, but Blake had never met her. He wracked his brain to see if he could remember what Lukas had said about her in the past, but the only thing he could remember was that her husband died a couple of years ago. Lukas had talked about how hard it was to watch her go through that.

Tess's shoulder's relaxed, and she let out a nervous laugh. "What'd she do now?"

Lukas rubbed his face. "Just riling up the local sheriff's department. We need to pay her a visit. Blake, you up for a short road trip to rescue my baby sister?" It might take a couple of days.

Blake grinned. "I'm always up for a road trip."

Anything to distract him from the hole in his chest.

# CHAPTER 2

Paige stared at the sheriff and his deputies. They looked at her like she was crazy. And maybe she was. But not about this.

Though she didn't know how else to explain what she saw. A man had been standing over her while she was asleep in bed. She'd screamed, and he'd run away. But he shouldn't have been able to sneak into the house without her hearing.

"Paige, can you give us any other indication of what he looked like?" Sheriff Randall asked.

She could still hear his footsteps pounding down the hall and the stairs. She shook her head. She didn't want to talk and hear the tremor in her voice. She hated feeling weak. This morning her horoscope had told her to be cautious in all her doings. Perhaps she hadn't been cautious enough.

"I've checked the doors and windows, and there doesn't appear to be any sign of forced entry. Did you lock them all?" Sheriff Randall had been the sheriff for as long as she had lived here. From what some of the locals said, he'd been born sheriff and would outlive them all. He was in good shape, but his wrinkles grew deeper every year.

"Yes." It came out more like a shriek. She was vigilant about that. Even when her horoscope didn't tell her to be cautious.

"We found the backdoor unlocked, but there's also no evidence a car has been here. Did you hear them drive away?"

"No." How could she? She was too busy hiding in the bathroom calling 911.

Sheriff Randall tapped his pen on his notepad. "Are you sure you didn't imagine it?"

She closed her eyes. Yes, she'd been having nightmares. And, yes, they quite often woke her up, but she wasn't imagining the creepy guy dressed in black standing over her. Even his face was covered.

It was far too real.

"No. I didn't imagine it."

"Then how did he get past your security system? I know you have a good one. It wasn't triggered," he said with exasperation.

"I forgot to turn it on." Actually, she didn't. She was tired of it going off every time she stepped into the kitchen in the middle of the night. She couldn't remember the last time she had turned it on. Dammit. She should've listened to her horoscope.

"Lukas won't be very happy to hear that."

She snapped her head up. "And why would Lukas need to know?" She couldn't believe Lukas had gotten to the sheriff. He'd always been meddling, but this was a whole new level.

The sheriff's cheeks flushed cotton candy pink. "He told us to call if there was ever any issues. So I called him before I headed over here."

"I can't believe you called him." She threw her hands in the air. She did not need her overprotective brother coming out here and telling her she had to move. He'd always warned her something like this would happen.

She *loved* her house, and she didn't want to go anywhere. The last time Lukas came to visit—six months ago—they'd fought the whole time about her staying here.

He hated that she lived alone in this big house where the nearest neighbor was a mile away, and the closest grocery store was a forty-five-minute drive. She didn't know how to convince him that she liked her isolation. He just didn't get it.

She opened her ornate wooden door. "Thank you for coming. Let me know if you find anything else. I'll be sure to set my alarm tomorrow night." Though the sky was pinking now. It was already tomorrow.

The sheriff and his deputy tipped their hats at her and left. She closed the door and sank onto the floor, her back pressed against the door.

Lukas would probably be here in a few hours. She had to think of a way to convince him that she wasn't going anywhere.

Nothing came to her.

At least he couldn't physically force her to do anything.

But he'd probably try.

# CHAPTER 3

It'd taken Blake and the others a couple of hours to get off the island and on the road. Everyone had to shower and pack an overnight bag in case they needed to stay.

Then they dropped Jack off with Hayden and Anna. Blake had nearly ditched Lukas to hang with them but wanted the drive more than he wanted to babysit. Anna would just want to talk about Debbie, and at this point, he was tired of talking about her. He pushed the thought of her out of his head.

"So what's the deal with your sister?" Blake asked as they drove down forest-lined roads without a house in sight.

Tess reached over and gripped Lukas' hand and Blake frowned. Maybe he shouldn't have asked.

"She's….fragile and kind of a recluse. And I don't know how to protect her. She flat out refuses any help we offer. I have a few people in town that keep an eye on her for me, but she's not super open with any of them either."

"Fragile, how?"

"I don't know how to explain it. When we were growing up, she was tough as nails, but then she married Emery and withdrew from the family. We still saw her on holidays and stuff, but she stopped calling me on a daily basis. I just thought it was because she was in love and distracted. She didn't need me anymore. I was busy with my own family so I didn't really notice it. Then Emery died and we all went to help out and it was like she was a stranger. She cried constantly and was scared of her own shadow."

"Grief can do weird things to people." Blake swallowed. He couldn't imagine how difficult that must've been for her. Sure, he was upset the love of his life just married another man, but the death of a spouse so young had to be devastating.

"They can, but that's just the beginning. The day after the funeral she was arrested for manslaughter. It was a car accident, and she'd run a stop sign. We hired the best attorneys and got her off on temporary insanity. Though to this day I don't understand how she got that. She never told me what caused the insanity. Anyway, instead of jail she had to do a couple of months in a psych ward. She hasn't been the same since."

Blake sat back in his seat. That was horrible. He couldn't believe Lukas hadn't told him this before. Though he supposed he never talked much about his family either. His parents had died when he was a kid.

"How often do you see her?"

"A few times a year. But I talk to her weekly and

threaten to visit if she doesn't call. She's gotten even stranger as the years have gone on."

Tess snorted. "It's true. She has crystals all over her house to ward off evil spirits and she believes the dreamcatcher above her head really does protect her dreams. She burns sage and grows a bunch of weird herbs in her greenhouse. She's always telling me what the stars and tarot have predicted."

Blake swallowed. Maybe he should've stayed with Anna and Hayden. Blake was fairly tolerant of people, but he couldn't stand people who acted like all the psychic stuff was real. He was firmly grounded in science and things he could see. He had no patience for silliness like that.

"I keep telling Lukas we need to find a good guy to hook her up with but he won't hear of it."

Lukas gripped the steering wheel.

"Why not?" Blake asked. It made sense to him and Lukas wasn't all that unreasonable. He'd never struck Blake as the overprotective big brother type.

"Because Emery destroyed her and I thought he was a good guy. In fact, I even encouraged the relationship when Paige had cold feet. When she asked me what I thought she should do, I told her to marry him. I never want to see her go through that again."

Blake didn't argue with Lukas, but he tended to think along the same lines as Tess. If he could, he'd be married right now even though it was risky to trust his heart.

"So why are we heading out there now?"

"Last night she called the sheriff about a break-in. Someone was standing over her. She lives so far out that if someone broke into her house, that meant they were looking specifically for her. I'm going to try to talk her into coming home. This is just one more reason she shouldn't be living so far away. I don't like her being alone. It's not healthy for her. She doesn't even drive anymore, so she never leaves the house. I worry about what it's doing to her psyche."

"Why doesn't she get a roommate or something?"

Tess chuckled. "We've suggested it. But Paige always finds a way to make it sound like a bad idea."

They drove down a long driveway and the house came into view. It was a monstrous log home but looked like it belonged in a fairy tale. There wasn't a straight wall on the house. Everything curved and twisted, and it had a gnarly roof. And even though the house looked unusual, it was the size that got to him. No one should ever live alone in a house that spacious. They'd go mad. Maybe that was why she was weird.

"You know, I thought your house was big," Blake commented as he climbed out the back door of Lukas's Navigator. Lukas's house was nothing compared to her home.

Lukas clapped him on the back. "The fudge fortune is good, but this house was paid for by Paige's husband. He was an architect and came from old oil money."

The house spread out in all directions, with not a single sharp edge. The porch was held up with what looked like trees surrounded by vines, and the front door was a double wood door carved with various animals. At first glance Blake spotted a fish, a fox, and a bear.

The house was a work of art, and he was insanely curious what they'd done with the inside. It was not his style at all. As a scientist and city-dweller, he preferred clean lines and a more modern style, but this had its charms.

Dio and Tria scrambled out after them and raced into the backyard.

"Are they going to be okay?" Blake asked, not able to see around the house.

Lukas nodded. "Her property goes down to the water. I always let Dio run when she comes here. As long as Tria isn't a wanderer, she'll be fine."

Lukas didn't bother knocking, just pushed the door open. Blake and Tess followed. The house smelled strongly of essential oils—which Blake expected, those who believed in horoscopes and things tended to believe in fake medicine.

Blake wasn't disappointed in the least by the interior. He stopped for a minute to determine the smell. It was lavender with lemon. He wasn't an essential oil guy, but as a botanist, he could identify the smells. The floors were made of natural wood in various colors, and like the outside, the floor wasn't straight lines. The wood ebbed and flowed like a wave.

An enormous spiral staircase with a treelike banister greeted them, and sculptures of trees and vines came out of the walls and sprawled along the ceilings. There was even a rock pond with koi in the hallway, surrounded by an indoor garden full of various herbs. Right off the bat, he could pick out fennel and chamomile as well as oregano, sage, and even dandelions.

Again, not his style, but he appreciated the artistry. On a shelf he spotted a diffuser in the shape of a large crystal.

They entered the kitchen, and it was more of the

same. All curves and lines with funky natural art and crystals everywhere. Blake was drawn to the windows in the back that overlooked lake Michigan. The house sat up high on a bluff, and sunlight bounced off the lake.

Lukas frowned in the kitchen. "Blake, can you grab Tess something to drink? I want to find my sister."

Blake opened the fridge and furrowed his brow. There wasn't a single fresh item in there, which didn't jive with the impression he'd gotten of this woman from her house. He expected all-natural organic everything.

But there were no fruits, vegetables, yogurt, or cheese. Nothing that could go bad. But lots of condiments lined the shelves.

"She's got Gatorade, juice boxes, or soy milk."

Tess made a face. "Soy milk? Yuck. Gatorade is fine."

Tess sank onto one of the uncomfortable-looking bar stools and patted her belly. "I should've stayed home. I'm not up for these long drives right now."

"I can imagine. Can I get you anything else?" He'd always imagined himself one day having a pregnant wife to take care of. He'd hoped that woman would be Debbie, but now he had to rethink that plan. He and Debbie always said they were going to have two kids and four dogs.

"I'm famished. I would love some ice cream if she's got it." Blake had never had siblings. He'd always imagined if he did, they would be the type of family that would feel right at home in any of their houses. The kind of homes where you could raid the ice cream without asking.

"I'm on it."

Except he wasn't. The freezer was completely empty save a few ice trays.

"No ice cream. Nothing frozen at all actually."

Tess creased her eyebrows. "This isn't like Paige. I mean, she was never a healthy eater, but she always had ice cream in her freezer. It's her favorite snack."

Blake stuck his head in the pantry. It was decently stocked. "Want some cookies? She's got loads of those."

"Sure."

Blake grabbed a package of Oreos and Tess attacked them.

Lukas came back into the kitchen, shaking his head. A voice followed him, but it was hard to tell what she was saying.

A girl entered. She was probably in her mid-twenties but looked younger. That was most likely due to her slight frame, but also because she didn't have on a stitch of makeup, and her curly brown hair was in tangles all over her head. She wore nothing but an oversized men's shirt that fell off of one shoulder and hung just past her thighs. The soft leaf-green button-down was rolled up at the sleeves and unbuttoned just enough that her cleavage peaked out.

It was dead sexy, and Blake forced his eyes up. He could not think about Lukas's sister that way. Though, this wasn't much better. He could easily get lost in her stormy green eyes.

"I don't need you always rescuing me." She stared daggers at Lukas and didn't even acknowledge Tess or Blake.

Lukas towered over her, his face going red. "You don't? I think you do. You can't live out here by yourself. It's not healthy and what are you going to do if someone breaks in again."

She propped a hand on her hip. "It was just a dumb

kid. I'm fine. I consulted the cards after the sheriff left and pulled the high priestess. I'm fine."

Blake pulled out a few cookies and resisted the urge to tell her that Tarot cards were fake. "What kid?" he asked, wanting to keep the conversation grounded.

Paige jerked her head around. "Who are you?"

Lukas nodded toward him. "Paige, meet Blake, one of my frat buddies."

She gave him a stiff nod. "What's your dog's name?"

"Tria."

Paige's lips' twitched. "Lukas beat you, huh? How?"

He and his nine frat buddies all got Dobermans when they hit their first million and named them in order. Hayden snagged Una, and Lukas scored Dio. But it should've been Blake.

"The drug I created got me seventy-five percent of the way there, and Lukas jumped in there days before I could make up the difference."

Paige narrowed her eyes. "Drug?"

"Yeah, I'm a pharmaceutical research scientist."

"You know, natural remedies are way better than those chemicals you're shoving down people's throats. Also, naturopaths that use muscle testing to diagnose are far better than all those invasive tests."

Blake opened his mouth to argue, but Lukas jumped in first. Which was probably a good thing. Judging by the smell of her house she probably thought essential oils and herbal medicines cured everything. As much as Blake knew the power of a good plant, he couldn't stand people who dismissed modern medicine like it was evil. Maybe his mom would still be alive today if she'd trusted her doctors instead of the herbalist next door. The industry wasn't perfect, but at least people didn't lose children like they used to and life expectancy was significantly better than it was a hundred years ago. Plus, with all of the allergies he had, he'd never be able to do his job without allergy medicine.

"Stop trying to change the subject. It's time to come home."

Paige clenched her tiny fists. "I'm sorry you drove all the way out here for nothing. That can't have been a comfortable ride." It wasn't a bad ride, but it had been long and Tess looked like she was about ready to pop.

Tess waved a hand. "It's nothing. What if that kid had a gun?"

Paige climbed onto the stool next to Tess. She clenched and unclenched her fists. "It was nothing. Probably just a teenager who was dared to break into the weird house. I'll be fine, and I'll remember to set my alarm from now on."

No one said anything for a long moment. Blake guessed Lukas was trying to come up with a better argument.

"Where's your ice cream?" Tess asked. "You always have ice cream."

Paige avoided her eyes. "I haven't been to the store in a while."

Blake snorted. "What like months? There is no fresh food in here at all, and your freezer is empty."

Paige dropped her head. "Amazon Fresh doesn't deliver out here, but Amazon Pantry does."

"I thought you caught a ride to the store with your neighbor," Lukas said. Blake wondered why she didn't just drive herself. Though he supposed if he ran a stop sign and killed someone he might not want to drive either.

"She moved, and I don't like the new one." Paige dropped her eyes and wouldn't look at any of them. Blake almost felt sorry for her because he knew how stubborn Lukas could be. Paige wasn't getting away with anything.

"That's it. You're coming home with me. Go pack a bag," Lukas pointed to the stairs.

The fury in her eyes flared. "I'm not going anywhere. You can't make me." She sounded like a petulant teenager. "Besides, Phil and Ida will be here next week. I'm fine."

Lukas pinched the bridge of his nose. "Phil and Ida travel too much. You need a better solution. You can't stay here by yourself. Can you get a roommate or something? Preferably someone who can bench press three hundred pounds."

"I can do that," Blake joked through a mouthful of Oreo.

Everyone turned to look at him.

"What? I can."

Tess squeezed his bicep. "I knew those things had to be good for something."

"No one's moving all the way out here to be my roommate, and I'm not moving back. There's too many people there."

Lukas scoffed. "Mackinac hardly has that many people."

"In the winter maybe, but it's the first of June. In two weeks it will be packed. You know I don't people very well." She clenched her tiny fists and looked down.

Lukas rolled his eyes and then pointed at Blake. "You know, in college Blake was a bouncer. He drives pretty good too."

"Wait a minute," Blake said. "What are you implying?" He wasn't sure how he suddenly got involved or why Lukas even thought she needed a bodyguard. It was one break-in and as long as she set her alarm, she'd be fine.

"You've got nothing going on this summer. You were just going to stay in the carriage house anyway. Why don't you stay here? Take care of Paige and make sure she stays safe and eats real food. Then after the tourist season is over, you can go home, and Paige can come stay on the island."

"You want me to stay with your sister?" Blake glanced over at her, but she sat quietly. "Do you really think that would be a good idea?"

If he had a sister who looked like Paige, and Lukas was single, he wouldn't trust him alone in the house with her. And Lukas was a better man than him.

Tess snorted. "She could do worse."

"You know I'm right here. I can take care of myself," Paige said, but Lukas ignored her.

"I'm not worried about that. I trust you. And I'll feel better if you're here on the off chance that someone breaks in again."

Blake swallowed.

This wasn't what he had planned.

But he couldn't think of a single reason to say no.

# CHAPTER 4

Paige couldn't believe they were doing this. She was never good at fighting with Lukas. He always won, but this crossed the line. Putting a man in her house. This was ridiculous.

"I'm not going to die. And I don't need one of your dumb meathead friends to watch over me." She eyed Blake. "No offense."

He raised his eyebrows at her, and she flushed. He was too good-looking. "None taken. But just so you know, I'm not dumb."

Lukas snorted. "That's for sure. He's probably the smartest one of my friends."

Paige pinched the bridge of her nose. That wasn't the point. "You're not pawning your friends off on me. Smart or not." Lukas was only a year and a half older than her and always overprotective. It's why she never managed to date anyone in high school. It'd only been the two of them, so they were close until she married Emery. They drifted apart after that. But once he died,

Lukas had returned to being the overbearing big brother.

"I'm not pawning him off on you. I'm offering you protection and a driver."

"I don't need it. It was probably a night hallucination. I'm fine." The more she thought about it, the more she thought maybe it was all in her head. Besides, she'd do anything to get Lukas to back off.

He crossed his arms and smirked at her. She hated that look. It meant he knew how to win the argument. "Either Blake stays here, or I'm telling Mom and Dad."

"Wait a minute, I haven't even agreed to this yet," Blake protested. Paige almost felt bad for him. But maybe he wasn't good at arguing with Lukas either.

"You will. Paige, which is it? Blake or Mom and Dad?"

Paige threw her hands up. If he told her parents, they'd come and stay here. And she was far more comfortable with a stranger than she was with her parents. They were good people, but they'd discover that she couldn't sleep through the night without screaming and hadn't for the past two years. Then they'd convince her to go to a therapist or take sleeping pills. After her stint in the psych ward, she never wanted to go near another shrink or pill again.

"Fine. Your dumb friend can stay here." Then she stomped from the room. She didn't want to see Lukas gloat. She stayed in the hall though so she could hear the conversation.

"That went well," Lukas said with a chuckle.

"You know, this is a gorgeous house with a view to die for, and I could totally appreciate this place for the summer. But your sister is nuts," Blake said. A jolt of embarrassment shot through Paige. She wasn't crazy, though Blake wasn't the first to accuse her of it. She waited for Lukas to stand up for her. She didn't want that dumb jock staying at her house. Not if he thought she was crazy.

"Oh yeah, she's always been a little high strung and a bit of a fruit loop, but since her husband died, she's gotten ten times worse."

A single tear ran down her cheek. Her brother didn't even try to defend her. Instead, he confirmed her worst fears.

Maybe she was crazy.

## CHAPTER 5

Blake had thrown his duffle in the back of Lukas's car when they left because he didn't know how long the trip would take, so he had no reason to go back to Lukas's house for anything. Lukas decided that Paige was safe and now that Blake was staying here, they wanted to get home to Jack.

Blake still wasn't certain this was a good idea, but if he had a little sister like Paige he'd want someone looking out for her as well. He just had to keep his thoughts brotherly. He had no idea how old she was. If he had to venture a guess, he'd say late twenties, but she looked much younger.

Paige bounced down the stairs. She'd pulled her hair back into a messy ponytail and had changed her clothes. Her eyes were red as if she'd been crying. His gaze floated down to her shapely legs. Brotherly thoughts were going to be difficult.

She glanced at his duffle bag and then glared at Lukas. "This isn't necessary."

Lukas leaned down and kissed her cheek. "Yes, it is. Remember the deal. Blake stays here or I tell Mom and Dad."

She pouted. "That's not fair."

"But you'll be safe and have food in the house."

Tess gave her a big hug and whispered something in her ear. She flushed, and Blake found he desperately wanted to know what she'd said. He was more than a little intrigued by this somewhat eccentric but beautiful woman.

Lukas opened the door and called for the dogs. Tria raced in and set herself at Blake's side.

They all said a few more awkward goodbyes, and then they were gone.

Paige stared at him for a moment, and he stared back.

"What's your sign?" she asked.

"Excuse me?"

"Your zodiac sign."

He rubbed the back of his neck. She was one of those. He shouldn't be surprised. "Virgo, I think."

"You think?" she asked with a raised eyebrow.

"I don't really care much about my zodiac sign." He was never one to care even when people were asking just for fun. But he was a man of science, not fake signs and all that.

She sniffed. "Well, then you are definitely a Virgo. I wonder what my psychic will have to say about this."

"Why would you have a psychic?"

"You mean you don't? I never make a decision without consulting mine."

Beautiful or not, no way in hades would he fall for this woman. She was about as opposite of him as things got and not in the good "opposites attract" way. He liked his women grounded and with an appreciation for facts —like science, not zodiacs or psychics.

"We still don't know for sure. When's your birthday?"

"September fifth."

"Yep. Virgo. I'm an Aquarius, we will not get along. But maybe if we sit down and talk about the differences between our signs we can work something out."

"Can you show me where I'll be staying?" he asked in hopes that maybe she'd stop talking about fortune-telling.

She turned and started up the staircase that still impressed the hell out of him. It seemed to float even though it was made of half logs. The spindles were all made of twigs and branches of various sizes. He felt like he was in a forest. Halfway up the stairs he stopped. "Are all those plants real?" There were dozens beneath him and hanging from the ceiling.

She nodded. "I don't like fake houseplants."

Maybe they did have something in common after all. "Anything that can hurt a dog?" He glanced down at Tria.

The plants he'd seen weren't bad, but he was certain there were things hidden amongst them.

"No. Everything is safe. Lukas brings Dio here, and I would never want to hurt her."

"You know I was a botany major in my undergrad work and then got my Ph.D. in medical plant science." They started down another winding hall which continued with the motif from downstairs. Someone had woven trees together then smoothed the floor out. He'd never seen anything like it before.

"That's impressive. But then you went and sold yourself out."

He resisted the urge to roll his eyes. "We can agree to disagree on that. What about you? What do you do?"

She pushed open the door to a room with a huge four-poster bed and wide windows with a great view of the lake.

"There's a bathroom through there. I'm sure you'll have plenty of room."

He would. It was a nice room, with a large king bed and a comfy sitting area. "Thank you. But you didn't tell me what you do."

"Oh, I'm an artist."

Of course she was. Anyone with a house like this would be.

He dropped his stuff on his bed and his phone buzzed.

*When do we get to see you?* The text from Anna wasn't a surprise. She was one of his best friends though they only talked once every couple of months. He planned on spending some time with her while in Mackinac, but now he was stuck here.

He didn't want to tell her though because he was afraid that she would take it the wrong way. She was always pushing him to find a new woman, and this would be too good of a setup.

*I decided to stay up here for a bit and explore. I'll come back for the fourth.*

*Blake! That's not fair. You were supposed to stay here.*

*I'm sorry. I'll see you in a few weeks.*

Tria bounced down the stairs in front of him. She hadn't left his side. She traveled well, but most of the places they stayed were apartments or townhouses, places she could easily keep an eye on him. Here, she'd lost him a couple of times and howled like mad until he called for her. Since then, she'd stayed right by him. He should've kept Dio here to babysit her.

After Paige showed him to his room, she disappeared, and so he decided to explore the rest of the house on his own. Almost every room had a stunning view of either the lake or forest. Outside he found a deck with chairs and a pool in its own little house with windows all around. He supposed it probably never got warm enough here to swim outdoors.

After he'd seen most of the house, he found another door that led to a basement.

He made it to the bottom of the stairs and was shocked to find a fully outfitted gym with a nice weight machine, an elliptical, and a barbell set. Dust covered the weights, so he'd have to wipe them down. And maybe find some oil in case the equipment hadn't been lubricated in a while. He'd find some at the store and set to fixing it up tonight, and then he could be back to morning workouts tomorrow.

He still didn't know what to make of Paige. She seemed nice enough, if not a little odd. But he wasn't sure if they would ever become friends or if they would always have an awkwardness between them. He hoped things would become easier. Otherwise, this would be a long summer. Maybe he needed to stop judging her opinions, but he couldn't help himself.

Who decided someone's character based on the day they were born? That was utterly ridiculous.

He tested out some of the equipment and then headed upstairs and into the kitchen. Paige stood there in a t-shirt and leggings. He didn't know who decided leggings were pants, but the entire male race owed them a debt of gratitude.

"Gym good?" she asked.

"Yeah. Your husband must've been quite a gym rat."

She shrugged. "Not at first. He only decided he needed to buff up a few years after we were married."

"You must've appreciated that."

"Not really. I liked him better when he was skinnier." Her hands gripped tighter on the mug she held.

Blake almost asked why, but then thought better of it. He didn't want her to relive painful memories.

# CHAPTER 6

Paige retreated to her art room. She wasn't being a good host, but she couldn't get those thoughts about her craziness out of her head. Plus, she didn't like having anyone else in her domain. Once upon a time, she loved hosting huge gatherings and having friends visit, but that all died when Emery did.

She closed her eyes and took three deep breaths like her therapist told her to, but it didn't work. She was out of Kava Kava, or she'd be downing the stuff right now. She made a mental note to order it this afternoon.

Her phone buzzed and she picked it up. Her group chat with her artist friends was blowing up. Those three ladies were her best friends, but she barely talked to them anymore. She did watch the chat though. Today they were talking about the upcoming retreat that she hadn't been to since Emery died.

She wasn't going this year either.

She glanced around the room full of over a hundred

of her half-done paintings. She hadn't finished a single one since the car accident.

She pulled out a blank canvas and squeezed black paint on her hands. She rubbed them together and stuck them down onto the canvas in a random pattern. Then she got up and washed her hands and went on the hunt for dry canvas.

There was one with an imprint of her leg and foot. She took a small brush and painted a flower coming off the top of her foot. She created more swirling flowers around the picture. It was nice, but definitely missing something.

"Nice studio."

She closed her eyes. Her solitude was once again ruined, thanks to Lukas. Maybe she needed to put a sign up that said *Do not enter.*

Blake would make fun of her art like he'd made fun of her interest in astrology. She didn't really have a psychic—she had to draw the line somewhere. She just said that because he was being so obnoxious about things. Sometimes when she wanted to get her brother off the phone, she did the same thing—started rambling about what her psychic said.

But she did put a lot of stock in the zodiac, her crystals, and her daily tarot card. Today she'd drawn the emperor card, which she hoped meant that she'd have more stability in her life. It could also mean a person who will bring balance and support, but there was no way a Virgo would do that. They'd never get along.

A dog nose pressed against her thigh, and Paige reached down and scratched Tria behind her ears.

She kept her eyes on the dog as she spoke. "Look,

you can leave. You don't need to stay. We just won't tell Lukas."

"I'm staying. Lukas had a point. It's not safe out here for you by yourself. Plus I could use a few months of R and R. So, I know you don't go out, but do you have people visit you?"

She raised her eyebrows at him. "You mean do I have friends?"

"I guess, yeah."

"I do. But they are snowbirds, so until they come back, no, I don't have friends."

"When do they get back?"

"Next week, I think. We spend a lot of time together in the summer. I can walk to their house."

She wondered what Blake was thinking. Maybe she could convince him that with Phil and Ida around he wouldn't need to stay. That didn't work with Lukas though and she had no reason to think it would work with Blake.

"Do all of your pictures have body parts in them?"

"Yeah, it's my signature. Body parts in every picture, though at times very well hidden. There are a few pictures that have left people unable to figure out exactly what is there." She missed finishing her pieces. But somehow, just as she got close, she could never figure out how to end them.

"Found your ear."

She turned around and looked at him. She was never comfortable around men like Blake. He was undeniably handsome, but it was his bulk that she couldn't stand. Emery worked out, but he had lean muscle. Blake was built like a bodyguard. Which she supposed now he was, but still, with muscle like that came overconfidence and usually a slight snobbery over artists and free spirits. His house was probably modern and city-like.

"It's easy when they aren't finished."

"Fine, show me one that's done."

"They're all in storage right now. But you can find pictures of them online."

He whipped out his phone. "And your name is?"

"Paige Heart."

"Using your married name, I see." Her stomach clenched. She should've used her maiden name when she started out, but she had really thought she and Emery were forever. It was too late now that she made a name for herself.

His fingers raced across his phone.

"Unfortunately."

He scrolled through a few pictures, but she couldn't read his face or tell what he thought.

"You're good." He squinted at a picture. Zoomed it in and zoomed it out. He spun the phone around and thrust it into her face. The painting was a bouquet of balloons, a simple picture, and she had made no attempt to hide that particular body part. "Are those your boobs?"

"Yep."

She expected a snide remark or two, but none came. Instead, he flipped through a few more pictures and then shoved his phone into his pocket.

"We need real food, and I need to get a few things to clean up the gym equipment in the basement."

She dropped her paintbrush in a jar of cleaner. "I'll shower, and we can go."

"Do you have a car?"

What kind of a silly question was that? "I have three."

"But you don't drive?"

She shook her head, not wanting to think about that. That stupid accident haunted her more often than she liked to admit. She rushed from the room and headed to the bathroom.

## CHAPTER 7

Blake took the keys from Paige and peered out the door into the garage. "A Beemer, nice." He always appreciated luxury cars, but he'd never been obsessed over them like some guys.

Paige shrugged and slipped on a pair of shoes. The doorbell rang, and she jerked her head around.

"I thought you never got guests," he said.

"You're wrong. I get one guest every day."

She left the garage and rushed for the door, and Blake followed her back to the foyer. Paige wrenched the large door open. A UPS guy stood there with a goofy grin on his face and a box in his hands.

Paige took it from him and set it down.

"Just one today. Looks like you're slowing down," he said, a tease in his voice.

Paige giggled, and Blake resisted rolling his eyes. He stood back, out of view from the driver. He knew he didn't literally need to be Paige's bodyguard, but at this point, from what he'd seen of Paige, she needed someone to look out for her.

"Naw, I'll probably have five boxes tomorrow."

"Then I guess I'll see you tomorrow." He gave her a wink.

"It's a date," Paige said with a giggle.

She shut the door, spun, and shook her box. She looked up and met Blake's eyes.

"Are you spying on me?" she asked with a glare.

"No. But I am tasked with protecting you, so I needed to make sure there was no one sinister at the door." He was being a bit dramatic, but he still hadn't been able to figure out the situation here.

She rolled her eyes. "Oh please, It's just Sammy. He's here like every day."

"He's in love with you." He didn't know why it bothered him, but he didn't like the idea of her hooking up with her UPS guy.

"Whatever. He's just nice. But he's a Libra, so even if did like me, we'd be very compatible."

"You want to date your UPS guy?" It was so utterly cliché.

"I didn't say that. I'm just saying…Oh, never mind. You're just messing with me."

She smacked him on the arm, and he chuckled, ready to let her believe it.

He wiggled the keys in front of her. "We should go, yeah?"

∼

BLAKE GRABBED A CART, and he and Paige perused the aisles. She snagged something from all the displays they passed and stopped at the berry table for raspberries and blueberries as well.

"Do you like smoothies?" he asked. There was no way in hades they'd be able to eat that much fruit before it went bad.

She shook her head. "But I love fruit salads. Oh look, I almost forgot the kiwis." She grabbed a couple of those.

"Are we eating dinner together and stuff?" he asked, the reality of their situation finally sinking in. He had to spend the entire summer with this woman who he barely knew.

"I think so. It's easier to cook for two than one. Plus, groceries would be easier if we just got them together. You're driving me around and staying at the house. The least I can do is feed you, so let me get the groceries."

She was being more talkative than she had been before. He wondered what changed. Maybe she was just happy to be getting real food again for once.

"I can pay for my own food."

"I know you can, but I'll feel better if I feel like I'm helping out as well."

He conceded. Lack of funds was not her problem.

He started grabbing various peppers and onions. "I'll cook sometimes though." He didn't cook often, but he had a couple of specialties.

"What do you make?"

"Stir fry mostly. I could eat it every night with different meats and sauces."

"Sounds good. But I'm not eating it every night." She raised her eyebrows in a challenge.

They discussed a few other meals, and she laughed when he told her that he didn't like potatoes.

"Everyone likes potatoes. Will you even eat French fries?"

"Nope. Not hash browns either." Or tater tots or scalloped or mashed. He'd hated them from the time he was a child. There was no rational reason for it.

"You're not human." She huffed.

"Says the woman who has been eating only non-perishables for months."

She snorted. "Truth. Oh, I want ice cream."

She spun and froze. A couple of women were standing there. One smiled at Paige, but it was definitely forced. Here he was beginning to think that Paige was a recluse who knew no one, but these two had obviously crossed paths.

The other one, a short stocky woman with long dark hair, waved. "Paige, we haven't seen you in forever. Where have you been?" Something about the way she behaved set Blake's hair on end.

Paige seemed at a loss for words and Blake figured these women were frenemies at best.

"We just got back from Japan," he said. He wasn't sure if he was doing the right thing, but he didn't think he had anything to lose. Debbie was always kind of a mean girl, and he hated it. She had many other redeeming qualities, but no one was perfect. Paige may be a little on the odd side, but he felt a strange need to protect her.

The tall woman narrowed her eyes. "And you are?"

"I'm Blake." He didn't offer any more of an explanation. He'd let them think what they wanted. "Paige, you were saying you wanted ice cream?"

She turned to him and nodded. He pushed the cart

forward with one hand, placed the other on the small of her back, and led her away.

"You need to breathe," he said. He'd never see her so wound up.

She let out the breath she'd been holding. "Thank you. I never know what to say to them. They're sisters, and they've hated me since the moment I arrived in town. But they pretend we're BFFs sometimes."

"Why?"

"I don't know. Abby, she's the tall one, is an artist as well. I think she liked being the only one in town. But I could be wrong. I honestly have no idea what I did to them, but they spread vicious rumors about me. Avery always follows along with what Abby does."

He grimaced. "I probably didn't help that. Sorry."

She chuckled. "No. It's a good thing they saw you. Perhaps the gossip will be in my favor now."

He chuckled and followed her to the next aisle. Several flavors of ice cream were spread out before him. He opened a door and reached for the Moose tracks the same time she did. Apparently they had the same tastes in ice cream.

"Maybe we should get two," he said.

"I agree." She reached for another one and then proceeded to get two more flavors—cookie dough and strawberry cheesecake. He appreciated both of them.

The summer might not be as lonely as he thought it would be. By the end of this they might even be good friends.

"What's up with all the junk food? No adult woman eats like this."

She chuckled. "Emery was a health nut and he was too tempted by this stuff, so I wasn't allowed to have it in the house. After he died, I guess I overcompensated. I'm a little addicted to sugar."

He picked up the things he needed for dinners. Chicken, beef, and spices for stir fry sauces. Paige found mostly junk food. By the time they headed to the checkout line, she had three different kinds of cookies in the cart.

"Oh shoot. I forgot milk. You wanna get in line, and I'll grab a gallon?" She waved him on to the checkouts.

"Sure."

His phone buzzed just as he was getting in line. He pulled it out of his pocket.

Lukas.

*How are things?*

*Good. Getting real food at the store.*

*'Bout time. No idea how she was surviving.*

*You and me both.*

"There is no way that man is her boyfriend." The nasally voice floated out from in front of him, and he jerked his head up. The two women from earlier stood in line not three feet from him. Both were facing forward though and didn't see him.

"I bet he's her brother or something. I'd heard he looked like a rock star." Abby sighed.

"I don't know. Did you see the way he was touching her?"

"Ugh. Maybe. They said they just got back from Japan. I bet he paid for the whole thing just like Emery used to pay for everything."

"Yeah, I'm surprised it took this long to find another sucker to support her crappy art."

"Right. I don't know how she landed Emery let alone a man like that. Did you see the muscles on him?" She made a low whistle sound. Blake rolled his eyes. Yes, he worked out, but it wasn't to get attention from women.

"Oh, I bet you're right. Maybe he'll stay in town for a bit. We can get to know him."

Abby waved a hand in her face. "That would be nice, but can you imagine having Paige as a sister-in-law? He has to be her brother. There's no other explanation."

He gripped the handle of his cart. These were the type of women who never grew out of that high school drama, who thrived on making others feel like crap.

He should defend Paige, but he knew nothing about her past marriage or much about her at all except that she was an amazing artist. The cart moved and he flicked his eyes down. Paige was dumping in a gallon of milk, a block of cheese, and several cartons of yogurt.

She gave him an apologetic smile. "It's been a while since I had real dairy."

The women in front of him whipped around and saw them. Their faces turned beet red. Blake still had no words to defend her, but one thing was clear. Those women thought that Paige was beneath him somehow.

He would show them that she most certainly wasn't.

Without warning her, he leaned down and kissed her.

## CHAPTER 8

Paige hadn't been kissed in a very long time and hadn't been prepared for it anyway, and so she barely had time to react. But as quickly as it began, it was over.

Blake moved to her ear and whispered. "I'll explain later."

She pushed the hair out of her hot face. Abby stared at her for a moment. There was a reason Abby hated her, and it had nothing to do with being the only artist in town. She just hadn't wanted to bring that part up to Blake.

Abby and Emery had become fast friends when he and Paige moved up here. They both liked to run, and Paige hadn't found it all that odd that they'd become running buddies.

The day Emery died, Paige had found out that he and Abby had been doing a bit more than running together. Paige was so angry about it that she barely even grieved Emery. She wouldn't wish him dead, but at this point, she didn't miss him either.

Abby had no idea that Paige knew, and Paige planned to keep it that way as well. That way Abby could never throw it in her face.

Avery giggled and turned back around. Abby wasn't quite as tactful. She kept her eyes on Paige, so Paige wrapped her fingers around Blake's waist and laid her head on his chest.

It was a fairly innocent move for a grocery store, but she was acutely aware of his whole body flush with hers. She tried not to appreciate how nice it felt. At least she didn't have to look at Abby now.

The sisters finished checking out, and Paige paid for their food. She waited until they got into the car to find out why Blake had made her lips burn.

"So, what did the evil sisters say that made you kiss me?" There was no doubt they'd been gossiping about her while in line. It's what they did.

He rammed a hand through his hair. "They acted like there was no way we could be together and that I was probably your brother or something. They were being so bitchy, and I just wanted to prove that you were not, in fact, my sister."

Paige laughed. "That was so worth it."

"But now everyone in town will think you have a boyfriend."

She shrugged. "It doesn't matter. I don't like anyone in town anyway. I don't really care what they think of me." And she didn't. She never had. She had a very tight circle of friends and the rest of the world could go to hell for all she cared.

"Surely you have some friends in town."

Before Emery died, she did. But since then, she'd

withdrawn and kept to herself. A handful of people blamed her for his death, and the others just didn't know what to say to her. And her isolated house made it easy to ignore her.

"Not really. Well, full-timers anyway. I was really good friends with my closest neighbor, but she moved a few months ago. There is a shop in town that takes my art, but I don't think the owner really likes me even though I make her a lot of money. I haven't given her anything in a long time anyway. I don't mind being on my own. Besides, summer is coming, and that means the snowbirds return. And several of them do like me. Phil and Ida are my other closest neighbors. They should be here next week. You'll like them."

Blake was quiet for a few moments. "So do you ever leave your house?"

"Not if I don't have to. Though I do enjoy being outdoors, so I walk on my property a lot or visit state parks. But when the snow is seven feet deep, I stay home."

"I'd go mad if I didn't have social interaction." He chuckled.

"I used to think that too. But things changed for me."

She wondered if he would ask what changed, but he probably already knew that. She wasn't even sure why it happened. She just couldn't stand being around people anymore. Deep down she wondered if everyone was lying to her and would betray her like Emery did.

Even if she knew that wasn't true, she had a hard time convincing herself it wasn't.

## CHAPTER 9

*A* piercing scream rent the air. Blake jumped out of bed with Tria on his heels and raced for the door. He stopped briefly to throw on a pair of shorts. Even in his sleep-deprived brain, he knew where to go. It was the one room in the house that he hadn't visited—the door firmly shut on his self-guided tour of the home.

Paige's.

The screams persisted as he rushed down the hall in bare feet and nothing but boxers, practically tripping on a rug on his way.

The door to her room was closed, and he shoved it open and flicked on the light.

Paige shot up in bed, her hair a wild mess. She continued to scream, her face screwed up and eyes closed shut. She clutched at the sheets on her bed in her paint-splattered tank top.

She must be having a nightmare.

Blake approached her cautiously, his adrenaline slowing now that there was no actual danger. After his parents had died when he was a child, he'd had nightmares too, and he knew what she was going through.

He sat on the bed and placed a hand over hers, wondering how often this had happened. She didn't respond. He crawled closer to her, put both of his hands on her shoulders, and shook her slightly. Not hard, but enough to try to get her attention.

"Paige, wake up," he shouted so she'd hear him through her screams.

She blinked her eyes open and closed her mouth. She just stared at him.

"You were having a nightmare. Are you okay?"

She looked over his shoulder and then collapsed into his arms, sobbing. Blake wasn't used to dealing with emotional women. Debbie had been the exact opposite, and he never got close to any of the other women he'd dated. He had no sisters and his mom had been stoic.

He slid up to the headboard, so he'd have something to lean against and pulled her with him. They were practically strangers, but he wouldn't let her cry alone.

He wasn't sure how long he sat there with her in his lap, sobbing all over his bare shoulder.

After a bit she sat up and sniffed.

"Sorry about that."

"It's okay."

Then her apple-green eyes widened. "Blake. Oh my word, I'm so sorry. I was half-asleep. Geesh."

She scrambled off his lap, and he chuckled at the flush in her cheeks. "I totally understand." He'd say anything in this moment so she wouldn't feel any more uncomfortable. Whatever was going on in her head wasn't her fault.

She stood off the side of the bed, her hands trembling. "Can you give me a moment?"

"Sure."

She raced away into what he assumed was the bathroom. Tria jumped onto the bed and curled up next to him. He flung a sheet over his legs so she wouldn't be too embarrassed by the sight of him in just his boxers. At least he'd stopped to put those on. He thought about going back to his room, but he wanted to get down to the bottom of why she woke up screaming.

Different colored crystals dotted the shelves, and on her bedside table sat a deck of tarot cards. She probably checked those every day and followed them religiously.

She came out of the bathroom, her face scrubbed pink, but she was still shaking.

He couldn't help but think that even a mess, she looked stunning. He glanced down at the tarot cards. Nuts. But stunning.

He was so in for it this summer.

## CHAPTER 10

Oh great. Not only did Paige wake up her house guest in the middle of the night, but then she discovered herself in his nearly naked lap, sobbing over his beautiful chest.

She was used to her brother and his friends running around with their shirts off, but she'd never actually touched a man who looked like Blake before. Emery was soft even after he installed the gym in the basement. He wanted to look buff, but he never quite pulled it off, and she'd been with Emery since her sophomore year in college. There had never really been anyone before that.

She didn't count the time when she was fifteen and played seven minutes in heaven and ended up in the closet with Hayden. Because that was just a sloppy kiss.

She wasn't usually attracted to men like Blake, but there was something about feeling the rippling of his abs under her hands that made her blush.

Now she couldn't stop looking at them. At least he'd

had the decency to cover his legs. But she wasn't sure why he was still in her bed. She sat across from him and pulled a pillow into her lap.

"Do you have nightmares often?" he asked.

"Every night. I didn't realize I screamed that loud. I'm sorry."

"Every night. Wow. What about?"

She didn't normally talk about the accident, but something about the sincerity in his voice and middle of the night delirium sent her words tumbling out.

"It's the accident. I relive it every night. The lights of the truck that slammed into us. The airbag exploding in my face. Emery's blood everywhere. Realizing he was dead." She swallowed the words now stuck in her throat. "Knowing it was my fault."

"How was it your fault?" He watched her with extreme concern in his eyes. She wondered if Lukas told him about this or not. Maybe he was just faking his ignorance.

"I ran the stop sign. Never even saw it. It was one I knew about too, but I was so angry, I just wasn't thinking."

"What were you angry about?"

She jerked her head up. If he heard the reason why she ran the stop sign, he'd think she'd done it on purpose. She was lucky she had a good lawyer or she'd still be in jail. "I'm sorry. I'm done talking. I...I can't."

"I'm sorry, I didn't mean to pry." His voice was so gentle. She now understood what Tess had meant when she whispered in Paige's ear. "He's one of the good ones, so don't deny yourself if the opportunity arises." This was not an opportunity. But he was being nice.

"It's okay. It's just hard for me to talk about." She wondered if it was just the middle of the night delirium, but she'd never admitted that out loud to anyone. People knew what happened of course, but she never talked about it.

"Is there anything I can do for you? A glass of water or maybe wine?"

She shook her head. "Thank you for coming. That means a lot to me." He could've just ignored her screaming, but he didn't.

"Anytime. Would you like me to leave Tria in here with you?"

"Yeah, that would be nice." She wanted to ask him to stay until she fell asleep again, but that would be weird. They'd only met this morning, but there was something comforting about his presence. His dog, on the other hand, was a good idea.

"She's a bed hog, but snuggles well."

Paige tried to focus on dog snuggles and not Blake snuggles. She reached over and grabbed a lighter from the side of her bed and some sage. She lit it and waved it around her crystals.

"What are you doing?" Blake asked.

"Clearing my crystals. They'll absorb all the negative energy from my dream and I need to keep them clean so they do their job."

Blake just stared at her like she'd grown horns. He opened and closed his mouth again.

"Okaaay," he said. "I think that's my cue to leave." She knew he thought this was all crazy, but if she didn't keep the crystals clear they wouldn't be able to help the next night.

Blake slipped out from under her sheets, and she couldn't help but stare at his retreating back. She slid back into bed, and Tria curled up as close to her as possible. Paige flung her arm around the dog and within seconds was fast asleep.

## CHAPTER 11

Over the next week they settled into a nice routine. Except the nights.

Paige woke up screaming every night, and every night Blake raced down the hall to wake her up. Her night terrors were epic. They never talked about it during the day though.

He barely saw her during the day anyway. He'd discovered a shed with all kinds of gardening tools and he lost himself in her yard. She said she had a kid who mowed, but the landscaping was a mess. The weather was too nice to stay indoors and the work was therapeutic for him. Maybe it was time for him to get his own house with a yard.

Most days he spent in the yard, though occasionally he went for drives to explore the area.

But they always had breakfast together and she always read him both his and her horoscope.

So far, the horoscopes had told him nothing. Though

he mostly ignored her when she read them, Paige managed to find truth in them every day.

"Ooh, it says you should start writing down your dreams. They might be prophetic."

He chuckled at that. She regularly appeared in his dreams—he couldn't help his subconscious thoughts—and she probably wouldn't appreciate it if he told her what they were.

"Mine says I'll meet the love of my life." She snorted. "Maybe you're right, and these are just a bunch of hooey."

"Who says you can't meet the love of your life?" He'd never heard her being skeptical of anything supernatural before.

"Because I'm never dating anyone long-term again. Once was enough, thank you very much. The love of my life could waltz into this room today, and I'd tell him he gets a summer fling. That's all." Blake found that attitude a little depressing, but truthfully unless the woman was Debbie, he basically felt the same way.

Blake sneezed, and Paige's eyes widened. "Are you sick?"

"No. It's just allergies. I've got Zyrtec up in my room."

"You shouldn't be taking that stuff. It'll just make you more allergic to other things. I'll put a diffuser in your room with eucalyptus oil and get you a bottle of lavender and sandalwood."

He gaped at her. "What are you talking about?" She'd mentioned this craziness before, but she'd never tried to force it on him.

"Essential oils treat everything better than pharmaceuticals." There she went again.

He sniffed. "Remember, I work for pharmaceuticals. I'll stick with my Zyrtec. I don't need that snake oil."

She sat up taller, her face scrunched up. "They are not. They are far better for you than the chemicals your industry feeds us."

The doorbell rang, before he could argue, and Paige jumped up.

It was probably that blasted UPS guy again. Blake had tried to answer the door a couple of times, but Paige always shooed him away. He didn't know why he cared. If she wanted to flirt with the UPS guy, that was her business.

Paige rushed for the foyer. Tria stared up at him. "I don't know what you're looking at me for. You know I don't feed you from the table."

Tria dropped her snout and whined. She was learning bad habits here. Paige constantly dropped things from the table "accidentally."

A squeal came from the door followed by loud voices. Blake got up to see what the fuss was all about. Paige had her arms flung around an older woman, and a young man stood behind them.

The woman let go of Paige and caught sight of Blake.

She giggled and approached him. "Who's Muscles here?" she asked, squeezing his bicep.

Paige kissed the young man on his cheek and rolled her eyes. "That's Blake. My brother insisted I have a bodyguard this summer."

The woman looped her arms through Blake's. "Ooh, a bodyguard, I bet you have good stories."

"I'm not a real bodyguard. I'm just staying here with Paige so she has company and a driver. I'm good friends with Lukas, and he didn't like Paige out here all by herself, and I needed a place to stay for the summer."

"Sure, likely story. I'm Ida, by the way. That's my husband Phil," she said with a nod to where Paige and Phil were talking animatedly.

Blake hoped his face didn't reveal his surprise. There had to be at least thirty years age difference between them.

Ida eyed him suspiciously. "Go on, ask the question. I know you want to."

Blake patted her hand. "I have no idea what you're talking about."

Ida let out a laugh. "Paige, I like this one better than Emery."

Blake met Paige's eye, worried that this might hurt her feelings. The blood had drained from her face. Paige hadn't so much as mentioned Emery to Blake, but he knew that was her dead husband. It was a little insensitive of Ida to say anything at all.

Phil rushed forward and stuck out his hand. "I'm Phil."

Blake took it, extracting himself from Ida. "Nice to meet you. I take it you're the snowbirds next door."

Phil chuckled. "Yep, my Ida is the most temperature-sensitive person I've ever met. Can't stand anything under thirty-two degrees or over eighty."

"Well, this is the right place right now. It's gorgeous. I don't know how anyone stays indoors."

Phil glanced at Paige. "You up for yoga again this summer?" he asked.

She grinned. "I'm always up for yoga." He should've known she'd enjoy yoga. All that meditation and stuff was right up her alley.

Ida put her hands on her hips and glowered at Blake. "You know a good host always offers his guests a drink."

"Of course," Blake said. "We've got coffee."

Ida winked at Paige. "Better make that an Irish coffee." She turned back to Blake. "Of course, a bloody Mary would be perfect too."

Blake's gaze flicked to Paige, but she just grinned at him.

"Um, I'm not sure Paige has tomato juice. I can get you that coffee though." He'd seen whiskey in the cupboard, so he could make that at least.

Blake made up a coffee for Ida, and Paige led Phil into her studio, chatting animatedly.

Ida hoisted herself up onto a stool. "I know what you're thinking," she said.

"What do you mean?" He was thinking Ida was a little over the top, but he still liked her. He couldn't tell her that though.

"Phil and a pretty girl like Paige disappearing into another room."

Well, maybe he was just into her weird art. His wife certainly was a bit on the unusual side.

"I suppose that is a little suspicious, but I just figured he liked art."

"He does, and Paige is his best friend. I expect they escaped to chat about you. Don't worry. Phil will fill me in when we get home."

"How did you and Phil meet?" He had to get the attention away from him and Paige. He didn't need meddlers this summer.

"He was my pool boy in Florida. It was love at first sight."

Somehow that didn't surprise him.

~

BLAKE MADE the mistake of inviting Phil and Ida over for breakfast the day after they arrived, and five days later, it had become a daily occurrence. Blake didn't mind. He liked cooking, and breakfast was his favorite meal.

Today, the door creaked open, and Tria raced from the kitchen to greet the couple and get the treat Phil always brought. Blake shoved his breakfast casserole into the oven. He wanted to be able to focus on the conversation with Ida instead of worrying that he'd put too much vanilla in his muffins.

Ida entered the kitchen in a flourish. "Where's my mimosa?"

Blake just shook his head and opened the fridge while Phil took his yoga mat to the space in front of the windows. He and Paige always did yoga while Blake cooked.

Blake grabbed the pitcher of mimosa that he'd prepped that morning and poured out two glasses, handing one to Ida and settling on the stool next to her. She took it from him.

"You must've gotten up early today." She raised her glass to him.

He clinked it with his own. "I didn't want to mess up the casserole, and you're distracting."

She flung her hair over her shoulder and batted her eyes at him. "Sorry, dear, I'm very happy with Phil. You definitely have a chance with that one though." She nodded toward where Phil and Paige were doing yoga.

Blake didn't even bother hiding his stare. All women were attractive in downward dog, but Paige especially so. She wore short shorts, and he totally enjoyed the view.

"Paige and I are just friends. If that."

Ida snorted. "Hardly. I see the way you watch her and her you. If you aren't sleeping in the same bed by the time the summer is over, I'll be very surprised."

Blake didn't take his eyes off of Paige. She moved easily into a standing position with her hands raised high above her head.

"That won't happen." Though he wouldn't mind. He could never be in a real relationship with her. They were too different, and she'd sworn off relationships, but she was beautiful. There was no denying that.

"Why the Sam hill not? Do you think you're too good for her?" Ida glared at him.

"Hardly. There are a lot of reasons. For one, I don't believe that the pharmaceutical industry is the devil. I like modern medicine."

"Oh phooey. Do you really think that Phil and I see eye to eye on things? We vote the opposite of one another in every election. I go to church on Sunday mornings, and he's an atheist. But we couldn't deny our chemistry, and neither can you two."

She had a point, but there was more to it than that. Lukas trusted him here with her this summer and he wasn't about to risk that.

"It's more than that. Lukas would kill me."

"I suppose you have a point there, but don't let him ruin your chance for happiness. You two belong together."

"No offense, Ida, but you don't really know me." He pursed his lips. She had no right to stick her nose into this.

She raised an eyebrow. Maybe that was uncalled for. Ida had managed to extract information out of him in the last five days. Phil and Paige spent a lot of time together, so that meant he and Ida just talked, and Ida liked stories. Blake had tons of them from his time overseas and traipsing through jungles. But she was also good at getting more nuanced information—like how his parents died and what it felt like when Debbie left him.

"I know enough," she said.

He wasn't sure that was true, but he wasn't going to deny it either.

## CHAPTER 12

*P*aige put her hair up in a ponytail and bounced down the stairs. She'd been feeling better in the mornings though the nightmares persisted. Perhaps she would finish a picture today.

She stopped dead by the kitchen. Blake's shirtless back was to her, and she appreciated a little too much the way his muscles moved. He shut the door and took a swig out of a Gatorade bottle. He'd been spending a lot of time in her yard and it actually looked decent for a change.

He spun around. "Oh, hey, I didn't hear you."

He smiled at her, and her stomach whooshed. She flushed. He was one of her brother's best friends and not at all her type.

"Sorry. I was just going to grab a drink and head to my studio." She needed to finish something. Anything. She was ready to get out of her dry spell.

He leaned against the counter, and she tried to not stare at him. "You've been in there every day this week."

"So. I like what I do." And she did, though it was frustrating at the moment. Something was off about every picture.

He smirked at her. "Finish anything?"

She scowled. "Not yet. Maybe today." Though she doubted it. She couldn't finish pictures that just weren't right.

"Why don't you come for a ride with me instead?"

"Where to?" If he tried to get her to go into town, she'd flat out refuse. She didn't want to run into Avery and Abby or anyone else again. Though she wouldn't mind if Blake tried to kiss her again. It'd been just over two weeks since he arrived, and she thought about that kiss daily.

She frowned. She couldn't think like that.

"Ida mentioned Kitch-iti-kipi at breakfast. I thought it might be kind of fun to check out."

"That's a two-hour drive." Being in the car for longer than a few minutes sent her nerves on edge. Plus, she didn't want to be trapped in the car with him. They barely knew each other and it would be awkward. Though she loved Kitch-iti-kipi. She hadn't been there in ages. She just wasn't sure she'd want to go with him.

"So?"

She shrugged. "It'll be an all-day thing."

"Let's pack a picnic and make a day of it. Come on, please. I don't want to go by myself."

She wasn't sure what possessed him to suddenly want to spend time with her. So far, he'd spent breakfast with her, along with Phil and Ida, and that was it. Most of the time he was out walking on her property and messing with her landscaping. She didn't mind. She didn't like working with her landscaping, just her herbs and most of those were inside.

Which was honestly for the best. Because otherwise she was afraid she might throw herself at him. Her feelings got all mixed up when she was around him.

But a picnic would be okay and she loved the lake. "I guess so." She didn't see how she could get out of it.

He gave her one of his grins. "Oh come on, you can be more excited than that."

"It's kinda boring and I've been there loads of times." It wasn't boring at all, but she couldn't very well tell him her trepidation was spending all day with him.

"But never with me. I'll be able to tell you all about the plant life in the water."

She rolled her eyes. "Oh boy, can't wait."

He ignored her insolence. "I'm going to shower. Do you mind packing the picnic?"

"Sure."

She would pack up the picnic and try to think what on earth they'd talk about all day.

~

"So, I still don't know why you are here," Paige said now that she had him trapped in the car for a while. She wanted to know more about his past. No normal thirty-something would hide away for the summer. There was a story there and Paige was determined to find it. She kept her hands gripped on the seat. Talking would be a good distraction.

"I told you, Lukas said you needed some company this summer, so here I am."

"No. Why were you even available to stay with me? Surely you could be out there inventing evil new drugs."

He squirmed in his seat a little. "It's a long story."

"It's a long drive. And if we're going to live in the same house together, we should probably get to know each other a little."

Blake sighed. "I suppose. It's because of Debbie."

"Who's Debbie?"

"The love of my life."

"Yep, there's a good story there and I want to hear the whole thing." This was way better than arguing about medicine.

For a second, she thought he was going to tell her to mind her own business, but he didn't.

"It's a bit sordid. Our romance isn't normal by any stretch of the imagination."

"Normal is boring," she said and Blake smiled.

"Debbie's older than me by about fifteen years. I don't care. She looks like she's about twenty and is smoking hot. That's not why I love her, but I needed to clarify that. I suppose it's a little like Ida and Phil, but not quite as extreme. When we met, she was my organic chem professor. Of course, lots of us were smitten with her. I booked every possible office hour with her I could. She was quiet, withdrawn, and a little sad. All I wanted to do was make her laugh. I never succeeded. Not then, anyway. The attraction between us was undeniable though. She freely admitted that. Night before the final exam we slept together. I got an A, and I didn't see her again for another three years."

Paige laughed. "You mean you slept with her for a grade? That's unbelievable." She wasn't judging him. It just didn't seem like something he would do. Though she supposed she didn't know him all that well.

Blake sighed. "No. That wasn't it. I wanted to keep seeing her, but as soon as the term ended, I went home, and when I got back in the fall, I went to her office, but she'd left. No one would tell me where she went."

"So I highly doubt you've just been mooning after her since then. You must've hooked up again."

"We did. Three years later she was my professor once again. This time it was grad school. She had a different last name, so I didn't know it was her until I stepped into her classroom. I'd walked in late, and she'd already started lecturing. She stumbled when she saw me. I was tempted to walk up to the front of the room and kiss her, but I figured that would be reckless. Instead, I took a seat in the very front row. The only one sitting there, actually. Drove her crazy. Course we slept together that night and every other night until I finished my Ph.D. We had to keep our relationship quiet, so it was mostly just sex. I took a job in South America when I finished, and we both agreed it would be best to just end it."

Paige clutched at her seat. "Was she married?" Maybe all men were like Emery.

"Divorced, I think. She never talked about it. I did ask her if she was married, and she said no. In love or not, I wasn't going there."

Paige heaved a sigh of relief. Not that it mattered. She wasn't going to get involved with Blake anyway, but at least he wasn't a cheater.

"You've had a career since then, so what happened next."

"A few years after that I took another job in Europe, consulting with a university in Italy."

"Let me guess. Debbie was there."

Blake nodded. "New last name again. This time though, I played things differently. You see, the other times we hooked up we couldn't date openly because she was my professor, but now she wasn't. Instead of jumping in bed with her, I asked her out for dinner. We dated for three months before we slept together again. I didn't waste any time after that. We moved in together and were happy for two years."

"Two years, huh. That sounds serious."

"It was. I planned on proposing. Had a whole scheme worked out. My buddy from Egypt flew up to Prague to help me pull it off. But she never showed up. Called me and told me she needed a break and met an Italian. She told me I could clean out my stuff from the apartment the next weekend because she would be staying with her new boyfriend."

Without thinking, Paige reached over and squeezed his hand. "That must've been hard for you."

"It was. I left her alone for a while after that, but I just couldn't stay away. Just before I came out here, I went to win her back, but discovered she was getting married."

"Wow. I thought I was the only one with a messed up story."

Blake chuckled a little. "Nope. I'm pretty messed up too."

Paige let out a breath. "Enough of this heavy stuff. Why don't you tell me a little bit about your travels? It sounds like you've been all over the world."

"Do you want to hear about the time I got bit by a Brazilian wandering spider or nearly drowned off the coast of Australia?"

"Both."

As they neared Kitch-iti-kipi, Paige realized that she hadn't minded the drive. In fact, the two hours had flown by. Blake had kept up a stream of stories of his travels.

The parking lot was empty, which was unusual for early summer, but it was a Wednesday. They parked, and Blake put Tria on a leash. She cowered away from him as he latched it.

"I don't think I've ever seen her on a leash." Poor girl. She'd probably love to roam free out here. She certainly did at home.

"She hates them. You'd think with as much traveling as we do that she'd be used to them, but she'd much prefer to run on her own. Once she gets a whiff of something interesting, she'll be fine."

They walked down the boardwalk and came around a corner. The idyllic spring-fed lake came into view, and a large boat sat tied to the dock.

"Come on," Paige said, excitement bubbling in her stomach. She hadn't felt this way in a while, but she was eager to see Blake's reaction to the water. It was like nothing else on this earth. Though she hadn't been all over the world, so maybe there was something like somewhere else and he'd seen it. She'd be so disappointed if he wasn't awed by it.

On the lake the single boat was available for anyone to board and take across the lake. It was on a rope that spanned the lake and when you turned the big wheel the boat went in a straight line along the rope and back again. It was only about a five-minute ride to the middle of the lake if you went slowly.

It appeared more like a flat barge, with a wooden roof and rails all along the side.

When it was busy a ranger manned the boat, but on slow days it was up to the passengers to figure it out.

She pushed open the gate and held it for Tria so she could get on the boat. Blake followed.

"You can let her off the leash if she won't jump in the water," Paige told him.

He did, and she grabbed the wheel to take them to the center of the lake. She cranked the big wheel slowly.

Blake glanced over the rail.

"Wait," Paige yelled.

"What?" He turned, and Paige was acutely aware of how close he was to her.

"Don't look yet. It's better if you get the full effect in the center." She wanted to see his reaction and the best part was in the middle.

He stared at her. "Then where am I supposed to look in the meantime?"

He took a step closer to her. His boldness surprised her, but she supposed it shouldn't after that grocery store kiss and how he'd stepped up to help her. She continued to crank the wheel to keep the boat moving, but there was an energy between them that wasn't there before.

She swallowed. "Just look at the trees. I bet you know what all of them are called."

He tore his gaze away from her, and the spell broke. She could still feel his body heat, until he leaned against the rail, looking up into the trees. Occasionally their elbows would brush together.

"Do you want me to do that?" He nodded toward the wheel.

She shook her head. "You can get us back. I like this part."

It didn't take more than a few minutes to get to the middle of the lake, and she stopped the boat.

"Can I look now?" he asked.

She nodded, and he moved to the center of the boat where a cutout had been made for people to view the lake bottom. Kitch-iti-kipi was one of the clearest lakes in the world. You could see everything. Large fish swam among the reeds and the sand bubbled up where the spring fed it.

Blake smiled and glanced up at her. "This is incredible."

"I know. I normally don't make it out here much because of the drive, but when I'm here, I could spend hours watching the fish."

"You and me both," he said. "But I thought you said it was boring."

She flushed. "I was just trying to get out of spending the day with you."

He mocked outrage. "Am I really that horrible?"

"No, but we don't know each other all that well and I worried it would be awkward."

"And has it been?"

"No. It hasn't."

She glanced down and watched the water because even though he said he could spend hours watching the fish, his eyes were on her.

## CHAPTER 13

"You want to watch a movie after dinner?" Paige asked. Things had been better between them since their trip to the lake a few days ago, and now they had easy conversations at dinner.

Though Blake refused to let her put a crystal in his room that ward out the negative energy. When she tried, he reminded her that she had one in her room and still had nightmares.

Blake quickly chewed and swallowed his chicken. Paige was a surprisingly good cook. Based on the kind of food he found in her house when he arrived, he hadn't thought she could cook at all.

"Only if there is popcorn." Their friendship had been growing and he enjoyed it. She woke up screaming every night, and every night he went in to wake her up. She didn't cry anymore though. Well, she did once, but she used Tria to sob on instead of him. Tria slept with her now, and Blake had hoped that would help the nightmares, but it didn't.

"Duh. No movie is ever good without popcorn." She winked at him and stood.

"I'll clean up, and you can pick a movie, but nothing too girly, okay?"

She giggled. "So no Hallmark movies for you?"

He groaned. Those were the worst, but Anna loved them so every time he went to their house, she made him watch them. "No, please not those."

"Well, it's a good thing you won't be around for Christmas then. I pretty much just leave it on twenty-four seven. They are my favorite."

Blake cleared the plates and stuck a popcorn packet in the microwave, then found a bowl and waited. Things moved much slower here, and he had a lot more time to just think. It was peaceful, though sometimes he wanted to get away from his thoughts.

He found it odd that even though his mind was free here, he rarely thought about Debbie. He was too distracted by Paige but didn't want to think about what that meant. Because Debbie was his future. Her marriage wouldn't last.

The popcorn quit popping, and Paige sat in the middle of the couch with Tria curled up next to her. Blake sat on her other side, where he could stretch his legs out long. He liked her couch a lot. It was U shape, and he planned on getting one when he got his own house. Something about being in her house made him think of his own. It was time to settle down. He doubted he'd stay here—it was too cold, but something like this, just farther south. Maybe Kentucky or Tennessee.

Paige reached out and grabbed a blanket from under the coffee table and popped a few pieces of popcorn into her mouth. She pushed play on the remote and stared up at the screen.

He should be watching the TV, but instead he found himself mesmerized by her.

Again.

He swallowed. This wasn't good at all. And quite frankly completely unrealistic. She was Lukas's sister, not his type at all, and still traumatized by her husband's death.

Plus, she would only ever be a rebound for him, and she deserved better than that. He scooted over an inch so their legs weren't touching, and she didn't even notice.

He finally drew his eyes away from her when the music from the movie alarmed him. The title filled the screen.

"Uh, I don't do horror flicks." He hadn't watched one since he was twelve and he didn't like thinking about why.

Paige jerked her head around. "What do you mean you don't do horror flicks?"

He grabbed the remote from off the table and paused the movie. "I can't watch them. I'll watch anything else, thrillers, fantasy, rom-com, drama. Hell, I'd even watch documentaries, but I'm not watching a horror movie."

She creased her eyebrows together. "Why not?"

"I just don't, okay? Pick something else."

He couldn't explain it. He shouldn't be scared of them. Nothing else scared him. He could tromp through the jungle with poisonous snakes and spiders, risk his heart for a woman who didn't love him, and climb on the sides of mountains a thousand feet in the air, but horror films weren't happening.

He shoved a handful of popcorn into his mouth and handed her the remote. If she didn't change the movie, he'd go for a run.

"I'll change it, but you have to tell me why."

He groaned. This was a story he didn't tell anyone. But if anyone would understand, it would be her. The knot in his chest grew tight. He didn't like thinking about this and he hadn't talked about it in years.

"My parents died when I was twelve. It was the middle of winter, and I had a few friends over to binge-watch the scariest movies we could find. We didn't have a lot of money, and it was a small house, but Dad had a mancave set up in the garage, so he and my mom went out to watch TV in there. Because it was cold they used a propane heater, but it wasn't ventilated properly. It was two a.m. when I found them. I've never watched another horror movie in my life." He hated thinking about that moment. Two years later his kid sister died from cancer and he'd been alone ever since. His aunt and uncle had raised him after that, but they weren't close by any means.

Paige didn't say anything for a long time. She reached over and squeezed his hand. "I'm sorry. No horror flicks."

He cleared his throat. It'd been a while, but sometimes the emotion was still raw. Paige kept her hand over his and waited for a few moments.

Then, she went back to the menu and flicked through a few more choices. She hovered over *Pride and*

*Prejudice*—the six-hour version—and gave him a sidelong look. Inwardly he groaned, but he didn't say anything.

She pressed play, and he settled in for a very long and boring night.

## CHAPTER 14

*P*aige blinked her eyes open. Sunlight poured in from the windows around her. She tried to move but found she was trapped. It took her a second to get her bearings.

She wiggled a bit, and a muscular arm held her tight against a rock-hard chest.

Ah, yes. She and Blake were watching *Pride and Prejudice*. The TV must've turned itself off at some point. She was on the long side of the couch with Blake, and Tria was on the other side, her snout only a few inches from Paige's nose.

She wiggled again, but Blake held tight.

"Blake," she whispered, though she didn't know why she was whispering. There was no response. "Blake," she said louder.

"Huh?" he asked and loosened his grip.

"We fell asleep last night." She wiggled out from next to him, stood, and stretched. He rubbed his eyes and looked around, like he had no idea where he was. It was kinda cute. There was no denying that she'd started crushing on him, but no way would she tell him that.

She knew he was still pining for that woman in Japan, Debbie.

"No wonder, considering the snoozer we were watching."

"We'll finish it tonight."

He groaned, and Tria climbed into his lap. "I'm going to hit the shower," she said. Because if she stayed here, she might sit back down and snuggle right into his side. He made her feel safe, and safe wasn't something she felt very often anymore.

She frowned and headed up the stairs. He was not a guy who would ever fall for her. He thought she was crazy, and she could never be with anyone who didn't believe in their sign.

She padded across her room and stepped into her stone shower. It was big enough for two people and even had an extra showerhead, but Emery had liked private showers. Blake probably would appreciate the intimacy of her beautiful shower.

She needed a good old ice bath to slow those thoughts down and then some serious studio time. She felt better today than she had in a long time. Her energy level was at an all-time high. She hadn't felt like this in a very long time.

Maybe this afternoon Blake would take her to the gallery to drop off a few pieces. She hadn't finished anything new, but she had a storage unit full of things she never thought were good enough to sell, yet now she just wanted to get something out there.

She lathered her hair and then her heart stilled. She

finally realized what was different. And it wasn't her attraction to Blake.

Last night was the first time since the accident that she had slept through the night and did not wake up screaming.

## CHAPTER 15

*B*lake's muscles were stiff. He should have never fallen asleep on the couch like that. He needed a bed. He might watch the rest of that sleepy movie with Paige tonight, but he was definitely sleeping in his own bed.

He wouldn't lie though. He could get used to waking up with her in his arms.

*Get a hold of yourself, man. This is Lukas's sister.*

Nothing was going to happen between them. He had to be professional about this.

He focused on breakfast and his guests. Ida helped him carry the plates out to the deck. It was warm enough out that they could eat outside.

He set his plate down and stared out at the view that he'd quickly come to love. "You're awfully quiet today." Ida placed a hand on his shoulder.

"Sorry, I've got a lot on my mind." Mostly just that gorgeous thing he couldn't have. But he didn't want to admit that.

She chuckled. "What on earth do you have to worry about out here?"

His eyes flicked to where Paige and Phil were finishing up their yoga. They both sat on their mats with their eyes closed and hands at their hearts. Paige looked absolutely serene.

Ida raised her eyebrows. "I see. What happened?"

"Nothing." He didn't want to admit the fact that they fell asleep together to anyone.

"That's a lie."

Blake rubbed the back of his neck. There was no one Ida could tell. Well, she could tell Paige, but he doubted she'd do that.

"Paige and I fell asleep together on the couch last night." He said the words in a rush, as if by saying them fast, she wouldn't react.

"And?"

This woman was good. He'd give her that. Now that he started talking, he was ready to spill the whole thing. "And maybe I'm starting to have feelings for her."

"I told you that would happen. What's the problem?"

Blake sunk down in the chair. "You know the problem."

"Debbie?"

His head jerked up. Oh yeah, Debbie. How easily she was being forgotten.

"Uh, no. I haven't thought of Debbie in days. It's about Lukas. He's one of my best friends. He'd kill me."

Ida took a sip of her mimosa. "Seems to me a brother would be happy his little sister found a guy who treats her right."

"I'm not that guy. I'm still hung up on Debbie, remember?"

"Oh please. Didn't you just tell me that you hadn't thought of her in days?"

"Well, yeah. But everyone knows that she's my weakness. She may be married now, but it won't last, and I'll be right here waiting for her."

"You mean to tell me that if Debbie were to walk through that door right now, you'd drop everything and be with her?"

Before Blake could respond, the door opened, and Paige and Phil spilled out, Paige laughing at something.

Blake could practically feel her body pressed against him every night like last night and bury his nose into her hair that always smelled like flowers. He wanted to taste those lips again, and he never wanted to leave here.

Oh, no.

This wasn't good at all.

"I believe I've proved my point," Ida said with a smirk.

Paige sat across from him, spread a napkin in her lap, and snatched a piece of bacon.

"What point?" she asked.

Ida waved a hand. "It's not important. I just like being right." Then she launched into a tale about her and Phil in Florida the year before.

Blake tuned her out.

He couldn't believe it.

She *was* right.

## CHAPTER 16

*P*aige sat closer to Blake than she'd done the night before, but she wasn't sure he'd noticed. She brought a big bowl of popcorn and waited for him to fall asleep because it didn't take long last night. As the movie went on, he sank lower and lower into the couch.

"I'm going to bed." He pushed himself up. The movie only had an hour left. She was actually surprised he hadn't fallen asleep yet.

"No. You have to watch the end."

He groaned, snuggled down, and closed his eyes.

Within minutes she was certain he'd be out. Once those eyes closed, he wouldn't open them again. She grinned to herself. She was being sneaky, but she'd had an incredible day today, and she was so looking forward to another good night's sleep. If she made it through another night, then she'd know it was Blake who kept the nightmares at bay. She'd probably have to talk to him at some point about that, but she'd keep him falling asleep on the couch for as long as she could.

She waited another ten minutes and then snuggled up next to him. She flicked off the TV and let her eyes drift shut. But she was far from asleep. She was utterly aware of his hard body at her back.

Desire burned in her stomach, and she was shocked at the feeling. Blake was so not her type. But he was sweet and funny, and she was falling for him.

Not to mention that she totally tricked him into sleeping with her again. He shifted behind her, and she worried that maybe he woke up, but he just rolled over and tugged her tight against his chest.

Her heart raced. There was no way she'd fall asleep tonight.

## CHAPTER 17

Blake understood what Paige was doing, and it had nothing to do with her feelings for him.

No, she was sleeping with him because she didn't wake up from nightmares. Last night and the night before on the couch together had been her only nightmare-free sleep since he'd been here. If he had been in her shoes, he'd be doing the same thing.

But he hadn't banked on falling for her. He wasn't even sure how he felt about her at the moment. He liked her a lot, and he wanted to see where things led.

But he still had Lukas to deal with.

The problem was, even if she had feelings for him, she was probably just looking for a summer fling. She'd told him before that she was done with long-term relationships after her husband. But Blake wasn't a summer fling kind of guy. He fell hard, and he didn't want to fall for another woman he couldn't have.

He spent the morning hiking in the woods around her house while Paige holed up in her studio. Just before lunch, Paige came out of her studio with two paintings in hand.

"You're not covered in paint," he said. She wore a light blue blousy top that revealed her shoulders, and a long white skirt. He'd never seen her so dressed up before and his heart raced a little.

She gave him a look. "I know. Would you mind running me into town today? I'd like to get these into the gallery, and there's a farmers market that I haven't been to in ages."

"Sure. Let me grab Tria's leash, and we'll head out." He had taken several trips into town alone and even explored some of the lakes, but in spite of him offering, other than Kitchi-iti-kipi, she never came with.

Paige jumped into the car and buckled her seatbelt. They took off down the road, and she still clung to the seat like she was going to die. But at least she was offering to go out with him more often.

"My horoscope said I'd come into money today. Hopefully that means I'll sell more of my pictures." She gave him a forced grin.

"You don't need money."

"I know. But I like knowing my art is appreciated." Even though it was unusual her talent was clear. He couldn't imagine her being insecure about whether or not people liked it. But he saw her point.

"I can understand that. What did mine say?" He couldn't quite believe those words just came out of his mouth. Oh, he had it bad.

She didn't respond, and he flicked his eyes to her face. Her cheeks were flushed, and she rubbed at her neck.

"I didn't think you cared about those things." She wouldn't look at him.

"I don't really, but judging by your reaction, I think I have to know."

"It said you would find true love today." She said the words in a rush, and Blake didn't know how to respond to that.

Then he chuckled to lighten the mood.

"Well, we are heading to the farmers market, and you never know who we'll run into there. Maybe my true love has been hiding up here in Michigan all along. But didn't yours say the exact same thing a few days ago? And you didn't find your true love."

Blake changed the subject and the rest of the drive passed quickly. It didn't take long for Paige to drop off her paintings, and the market was right downtown.

He parked the car, forced a wiggling Tria to stand still so he could hook up her leash, and crossed the street with Paige. For a small town, the market was pretty busy.

Paige stopped dead on the sidewalk.

"What?" Blake asked.

"It's Abby and Avery."

Blake followed her eye line. Sure enough they were staring right at him again. He'd never understand women, but he knew how to help Paige out on this one.

He grabbed her hand and wove his fingers through hers. "Don't mind them. We can totally act like we're in love."

Paige nodded and leaned into him. He appreciated it way too much. He had no idea why those two bothered her so much, but he'd get to the bottom of that eventually.

For now, the weather was gorgeous, he had his arm around a woman he was quickly falling for, and he had a market full of his favorite foods to explore.

Life was good.

## CHAPTER 18

The night before, Paige had managed another nightmare-free sleep. This was incredible, but she didn't think Blake would fall for it again. Still, she had to try.

At the farmers market, they grabbed several fresh veggies and spent the rest of the day together. At dinner, they made eggplant lasagna. This was becoming more and more common, and Paige liked Blake's company.

They finished cleaning up the dishes, and Blake snapped her on the behind with the towel.

"Hey." She snatched it from him. "This is not the guys' locker room."

He shrugged. Her palms were sweaty because she was afraid he would see right through her.

"You want to watch another movie? Your choice this time," she offered.

He leaned against the counter, crossed his arms, and stared at her. "No. I don't. Can we take a walk by the water instead?"

"Um, I guess." She really didn't want to spend the night alone, but she didn't know how to tell him that.

She followed him across her grass and onto the sand. He sat down, away from the water, and Tria took off across the sand.

Tria found a stick and raced toward them. She dropped it, and he threw it for her.

"She likes it here," Blake said.

"She's a good dog. I've never had one before." Nerves settled in her stomach. She didn't know what he was about to say.

He chuckled. "She likes you."

"I'm glad."

"So, about the couch."

Oh, no. He had seen right through her. She was about to be humiliated.

"It's okay. We don't need to talk about it." Her words came out in a rush, and she stared off into the woods so he couldn't see her hot face.

"Actually we do. I know what you're doing. You might not have intended it the first night or maybe even last, but now you're going for three in a row. Either you really like me, and you're afraid to say something, or you just really enjoyed not waking up from awful nightmares. My money is on the second one. Though if it's the first, I wouldn't complain. Your brother might though."

What was he saying? That he liked sleeping with her, and that he wanted more? This got complicated fast. She wasn't sure what she felt about him, but if he leaned over and tried to kiss her right now, she'd definitely let him.

But he didn't.

She faced him. "Lukas has no say in who I spend my nights with. But you are correct, it is the second one. I haven't had a full night's sleep since the accident. Well, until two nights ago anyway. It was nice. I would think it was the couch, but I slept out there for the first two months after the accident, and I still had nightmares." She wasn't about to admit how much she wanted him. This was hard enough as it was.

"Well," he huffed. "I'm not sleeping on the couch anymore."

She let out a breath. She understood. She didn't like it, but she understood. "That's fine. I get it."

"No, I wasn't done. I am willing to join you in bed, completely innocently, if you want. That way we both get to sleep, and I don't wake up with sore muscles."

This was scary and a little bit weird, but she wasn't opposed to the idea. She'd figured if they fell asleep on the couch enough, it would eventually go there anyway. But she'd just thought it would naturally migrate that way, not that they would have to talk about it. She was so not comfortable with the talking part.

"Okay. That would work. Thank you."

He reached over and squeezed her hand. "I'm here to protect you even if that means protecting you from the things in your head."

"That means a lot to me. I never knew Lukas had such cool friends. Well, Hayden I know, but not the rest of you."

"Oh, shoot. That reminds me. Fourth of July is in a couple of weeks."

"Yeah, so?"

"So, we all get together. You wanna come?"

"Where?" Lukas had mentioned these trips before.

"Mackinac this time. We wanted to keep it local this year with all the pregnancies and stuff."

"How long will you be gone?" She'd gotten used to his company and even though she fought it at first, she didn't want to be alone in the house again.

"Just the weekend."

She couldn't go a whole weekend without him now, go back to no sleep again. This was not good at all.

"Um, yeah, I think I'll come. Mom and Dad have wanted me to visit anyway." She rarely went back to the island. She loved her family, but they were overbearing.

"Then it's settled."

∼

PAIGE CREATED a wall of pillows between her and Blake. She didn't want him getting the wrong idea. Not that it would be the wrong idea. She'd finally admitted to herself that her feelings for him went beyond just enjoying his protection. She was falling hard for him.

Which was strange. She'd never really fallen like this. Sure, she was in love with Emery, but that had been such a gradual thing she'd barely even noticed. But he never made her skin tingle the way Blake did or made her heart race when he walked into the room.

However, she couldn't get a read on Blake at all. She knew he was attracted to her, but she figured that was more in the vein of "I'd like to sleep with you and never see you again after the summer." Which would crush her. That was not her style at all. She'd only ever slept with Emery, and she just wasn't the person for one-night stands and such. Although she'd joked early on with Blake about summer flings, she hadn't meant it.

But she'd just never considered truly staying celibate for the rest of her life.

No. Definitely, not. That thought was ridiculous at her age.

So either she had to get comfortable with casual sex, or she had to let her guard down and fall in love again.

Neither one of those sounded appealing to her.

She slid into bed and felt it move as Blake did as well. She flicked off the light on her nightstand and tried to close her eyes. But instead she stared at the wall of pillows.

"Is this weird?" she asked. It was totally weird. Her best friend, Stormy, would totally laugh at her for this. It'd been a long time since she confided anything to Stormy.

For some reason though, this didn't feel that weird. Because it was Blake.

He poked his head over the pillows, and she could barely make out his features in the moonlight. She would die and go to heaven right now if he leaned over and kissed her.

But he didn't.

Again.

And she was surprised at how frustrating that was.

"A little. You've been through something that I can't even comprehend. I've been through my own crap. Remember I can't watch horror movies because of my parents. It's okay. I get it."

"Thanks again." She was grateful he didn't think this was too weird. She was just glad she was getting some sleep.

"Don't mention it."

He dropped back down on his side of the pillows,

and before long, she heard his breathing change to long deep breaths.

~

BLAKE DIDN'T KNOW what happened to the pillow shield in the middle of the night, but he woke with Paige's head on his shoulder, her hand resting a little too low on his stomach, and a leg flung over his.

She would be embarrassed if she realized she was practically on top of him, but he couldn't wiggle out from underneath her without waking her. He let his fingers absentmindedly play with her hair.

This was something he never had before. Debbie was not a cuddler. After sex, she always stayed firmly on her side of the bed, and if he tried to get close to her, she'd shoo him away. Even when they watched movies together, the most she would do was hold hands.

Not that Debbie had been the only woman he'd been with, but the others were short, one-night-type things.

This kind of intimacy was new to him, and he was not supposed to be intimate with her at all.

Time to get up. Before he let his mind wander to other things he'd like to do with her.

He shifted his weight and slid a couple of inches to the left, but the hand on his stomach suddenly came to life. She clawed lightly at his skin.

"Don't go," she muttered.

Holy hell he was in a world of trouble.

## CHAPTER 19

"Are you even awake?" Blake asked. Paige shimmied herself closer to him, pressing her chest into his bare ribs. She was awake, but still a little brain fogged from sleep. She wanted to stay right here in his arms for a bit longer.

"I am."

"And you are aware that you are manhandling me?"

She chuckled. "Like you aren't loving this. I had no idea you slept shirtless." She was trying to remember why she wasn't open with him about her feelings, but at this moment in time, she saw no reason to.

He continued to play with her hair, and she nearly drifted off again.

"We can't do this," Blake said.

"Why not?" she mumbled.

"Because you are Lukas's little sister."

"So." She was so warm and comfortable, she didn't want to move. This was blissful.

"So, I don't want to get punched in the nose for taking advantage of you."

She sniffed. "Oh, please, we'll just tell him I took advantage of you, which is actually more of the truth. I lured you to my bed, and then, how did you put it? Manhandled you." She chuckled at her own joke.

He slid out from underneath her, and she pulled the pillow he was using into her arms instead. She inhaled. It smelled like him. He left without another word, and she fell back into a deep sleep.

~

PAIGE WOKE with a start and grabbed her phone. It was after ten. She never slept that long. She scrambled out of bed and jumped into the shower. Getting a full night's sleep was the best thing that had happened to her in a long time.

She was glad Blake had agreed to help her, even if the situation was a little weird. Somehow she'd ended up on his side of the bed, and his scent was all around her. It was musky and manly with a hint of that cologne he always wore. He'd starred in all her dreams the night before. She blushed as she thought of them.

She didn't know what she would do at the end of the summer when he left, but she didn't need to worry about that now. She had another eight weeks. Eight weeks of glorious sleep.

She brushed out her hair, pulling it into a ponytail, and threw on a tank and yoga pants. Then she jogged down the stairs.

Blake was in the kitchen, and he smiled at her. "Hey,

you're awake. I nearly came up there to check if you were still alive."

She hopped up on the counter and sat, facing him, while he put flour and eggs into a bowl. Before she knew him, she'd never pegged him as someone who baked, but his blueberry muffins were to die for. She'd told him so yesterday.

"I slept amazingly. Thank you. I have more energy today than I've had in weeks."

He chuckled. "Good. I slept much better last night than I had on the couch."

"It wasn't too weird?"

He looked down into the bowl where he was stirring the batter. "With the exception of this morning, no, it wasn't too weird."

She plopped a blueberry that had not made it into the batter into her mouth. "What happened this morning? I wasn't snoring or anything, was I?"

He set down the bowl and stared at her. "You really don't know what I'm talking about?"

Her insides went cold. What the hell had she done?

"No, but I need you to tell me." In her place between dreams and wakefulness, she often had times where she wasn't sure what was real and what was a dream. It'd always been like that. If she'd done something embarrassing, she had to know.

He chuckled and poured the blueberries into the bowl. "Oh no. If you don't remember, I'm not telling you."

Her mind raced through possibilities. "Did I drool on you?"

His lips twitched. "In a manner of speaking."

She shoved his arm and met the hard muscle. Her

mind flashed back to her dream. The one starring him and his glorious chest and abs. "Tell me what happened."

"Give me a minute here." He took his time and poured the batter into a muffin tray and popped it into the oven. Then he came and stood directly in front of her, placing a hand on either side of her. If they were together, she would've reached out with her legs and drawn him closer, but they were just friends. Or something. She wasn't even sure what they were.

"You really want to know?"

"I do."

"It's going to embarrass you." His eyes twinkled.

She dropped her eyes. "So embarrassing that you won't sleep with me again?"

He chuckled. "No. It'll take a lot more than that."

She placed a hand on his chest. "Just tell me already."

"You were sleeping on my chest this morning, and when I tried to get away without waking you, you told me to stay."

She jerked away from him, her stomach flooding with dread. That was part of her dream. Or at least she'd thought it was. But the dream had progressed much further than just lying on his chest.

Their kiss. But it was just in her dream. Wasn't it?

Oh no. She swallowed audibly.

"I thought that was just a dream. How far did it go?"

He raised an eyebrow. "How far did it go in your dream?"

She was not telling him that. "Uh-uh. You have to answer my question."

He moved away from her and leaned on the counter next to her, grabbing an apple from the bowl and taking a big bite of it. "It didn't. I told you we couldn't do anything because of Lukas, and you pouted a bit. Then I got out of bed, and you fell asleep. I really thought you were awake. Phil and Ida have already been here, and we had bacon and eggs. I was actually making the muffins as a peace offering because I figured you were too embarrassed to face me."

"I am now." She kept her gaze averted. She wasn't sure she'd ever be able to look at him again.

He shrugged. "You shouldn't be. For the record, the feeling is mutual, but I won't risk my friendship with Lukas over a few weeks of good sex."

He might not be willing to, but she certainly would.

## CHAPTER 20

*Blake* wasn't sure what possessed him to say that. He checked on the muffins, but they weren't done yet, so he couldn't use them as a distraction.

"Sorry. I didn't mean to make things awkward," he said.

She smiled at him, and it took all the self-will he had not to go there and kiss her. He nearly had earlier, but he meant what he said. His friendship with Lukas wasn't worth this. In the end, he'd lose both of them.

She whipped out her phone. "Let's see what our horoscopes say. If they say anything about true love, then we let the muffins burn and go back upstairs to bed. If they don't, we'll just pretend like this awkwardness never happened. Sound good to you?"

He should've said no. But his hormones overrode his brain. "Sure, we'll consult the stars."

Before she could read them, the doorbell rang, and

she jumped off the counter. He followed, knowing full well it was the UPS driver he couldn't stand.

Paige flung open the door, and the idiot on the other side beamed at her. Blake rolled his eyes.

"What'd you order this time?" Sammy—that was his name—set the box just inside the door, and Paige leaned against the frame.

"You know I never tell."

Blake couldn't see her face, but her tone was very flirtatious.

"Come on, just this once."

Nope, he wasn't going to let her continue this stupid conversation with this dimwit. He snuck up behind her and slipped his arm around her waist, tugging her close to him. She squeaked.

"Hey, Sammy, how's it going." Blake forced a smile on his face.

Sammy gulped and stared up at him. "F...f...fine."

"Betcha got a lot more deliveries to make." Paige had stiffened in his arms. Blake kept his tone easy going.

"I...I...do."

"Well, we wouldn't want to keep you," he said and pulled Paige into the house. "Have a nice day."

He shut the door quietly.

Paige punched him on the arm, her face full of indignation. "What was that all about?"

"He was flirting with you."

"So?"

"So." He stared at her for a moment and realized that maybe he'd read her all wrong. She seemed really upset. "So, I thought we were about to see if our horoscopes said were meant to be."

"You don't believe in that stuff." She pursed her lips and backed away from him.

"But you do."

"And maybe my horoscope is about Sammy."

He creased his eyebrows. Wait, what? How did this go from about him to Sammy? "I'm confused."

"Maybe Sammy doesn't care about my brother. Maybe I should go after him instead of you." She crossed her arms and glared at him. He wasn't sure if she was really mad or just messing with him.

"Oh, so now you're going to date him?" Blake didn't know why this bothered him so much. It shouldn't.

She lifted a shoulder. "Maybe I should. It's time for me to get out there again, and he's a nice guy. It's not like I have any other prospects."

She was taunting him, and he was falling into her trap. He couldn't figure out what she wanted.

His timer beeped, and he raced to the kitchen.

## CHAPTER 21

Paige needed Blake to stop giving her mixed signals. She was baiting him with Sammy, and she thought that would make him finally admit how he felt about her, but instead he ran away.

She marched into the kitchen and caught a nice view of his backside as he bent over to pull the muffins out of the oven. She had the urge to smack it, but she wasn't sure they were at that level yet.

How she wanted to be though.

He set the pans on the top of the stove and examined them. She stood next to him and crossed her arms.

"I'm tired of this," she said. This dancing around was ridiculous. They had eight weeks of summer left, and they'd never survive the tension without something happening. So something needed to happen.

"Of what?"

"Of pretending like we aren't madly attracted to each other." She hopped back on the counter so she was facing him. "We've got eight weeks. Let's make the best of them."

He crossed his arms and slid closer to her. "And what happens at the end of the eight weeks?"

"You leave, and I move back to Mackinac." She wouldn't really move back, but right now that's what Lukas thought and so she'd keep up the charade, but she was never leaving.

"What if I don't want to leave at the end of the eight weeks?"

She jerked her head around. "What's that supposed to mean?"

"It means, I'm not a summer romance kind of guy. I fall pretty hard. What if I fall for you?"

She dropped her eyes. She wasn't prepared for that kind of response. "I thought you weren't into hippy artists."

He chuckled and brushed a strand of hair behind her ear, his fingers leaving a blazing trail on her cheek. "I'm not. But I might make an exception for you."

She flushed. "I don't know. You know I'm not really interested in anything long-term." Never again did she want to put herself in a position of getting hurt. But maybe she was. Blake was…different than any other guy she'd known.

He nudged her knee. "Come on, don't be all embarrassed. I'm glad we're clearing the air. We needed to. I like you, I'm not going to lie. I think you're incredibly hot. You make me laugh, and you make me think. Plus you're amazingly talented at a lot of things, tough as nails, but also incredibly vulnerable."

He moved in front of her, and her heart raced. She

stared at his chest because she didn't dare look him in the eyes. She clutched at his shirt, and he hissed.

"Then why don't you do something about it?"

She finally met his eyes and saw torment there.

"Because you're Lukas's sister, and he trusted me here with you. I'm not about to break that trust." He set his hands on the counter on either side of her. "Not gonna lie though. The thought of you with any other guy makes me want to punch something."

She chuckled. "We're not going to be able to hold out all summer. You know that. There's too much chemistry."

"Speak for yourself. I have the willpower of a monk. I'm used to seeing what I want and not getting it." He pursed his lips and frowned.

He let go of the counter and sauntered from the room. Paige stared after him wondering what on earth happened to him that made him so strong.

Tormented, but strong.

## CHAPTER 22

That night, Blake grabbed Tria's leash when he saw Paige stretching and yawning. It took all of his willpower to not go over and kiss her.

Clearing the air between them was a good thing, but now he knew exactly what she wanted, and he couldn't have her.

But damn if he didn't want her.

He didn't know how they would manage to sleep in the same bed together and not have something happen.

"I'm taking Tria for a walk," he said.

Paige glanced up at him. "So late?" It was nearing ten.

"I'm not tired, and I'm going a little stir crazy." He worried that she might offer to come with, but he needed time away from her.

She nodded. "Okay. I'm going to bed. I'll see you in the morning."

Blake took Tria down the street past Phil and Ida's house. The lights were off, which was a shame, because

Blake might've stopped by and chatted with them for a while.

As he circled back, he wondered if Paige was right. They probably wouldn't last without something happening. But his feelings were all mixed up. He was falling for this crazy girl, and he didn't know why.

She was everything he never wanted. She was new agey and artsy. She believed in psychics and astrology.

And yet, he didn't see her as someone he just wanted to sleep with because she was pretty with a nice body. He wanted to love her.

He came around a corner, and Tria spotted a squirrel and practically yanked his arm out of the socket. He pulled her back, and she whined.

She couldn't have what she wanted either. He jammed a hand through his hair.

He had a feeling that before this summer was over, he'd have more than his fair share of drama.

And he couldn't figure out what he was waiting for.

If it would happen eventually, why not enjoy it while he could?

## CHAPTER 23

*P*aige woke late the next morning. Blake was gone, and the wall of pillows between them remained intact, but the sheets on the other side had definitely been disturbed, so he'd slept there. Besides, she hadn't had any nightmares.

She skipped down the stairs, but didn't see Blake or Tria anywhere. The front door opened.

"Yoo-hoo, are you two lovebirds up?" Ida called.

"Come on in," Paige yelled back.

She entered the kitchen and found it strangely dark. She flicked on a few lights. A plate of muffins sat there and a dish covered in tinfoil, with a note on top.

*Went for a drive. Won't be home until late. The casserole needs to cook for thirty minutes at 350. Tell Ida and Phil that I'm sorry I missed them. There is a pitcher of mimosas in the fridge. -B*

Paige turned on the oven and popped the casserole in, trying to ignore the sense of dread settling in her stomach. Blake had never left without talking to her before. He'd gone on drives alone, but he'd always asked her to go with first. She wasn't sure what to make of this.

"Where's Blake?" Ida sat on a stool with a flourish while Phil went to set up the yoga mats.

Paige forced a smile. "He's off touring today."

Ida raised an eyebrow. "And you didn't want to go with?"

"No. I want to work on some paintings today." She wasn't going to open up and confess that she really did want to go with him. She missed him.

"Hmph. Okay. Well, I still want my mimosa."

∽

PAIGE WAS RARELY LONELY. She'd lived for nearly two years alone before Blake showed up, and she always managed to amuse herself. But the house felt empty all day long. She worked on her art, cleaned up, and went on two walks.

When the sun finally set, she turned on a movie.

Blake still hadn't come home.

At midnight she finally went to bed.

## CHAPTER 24

The last week had been pure torture for Blake. Ever since their conversation in the kitchen where he nearly kissed her, he'd successfully avoided her. They still slept in the same bed, but he waited until she fell asleep and slipped away before she woke, going on long drives and walks.

He'd found her entangled with him a few times, but she always slept through the unentangling.

And now they were heading to Mackinac, and he could face Lukas with a clean conscience.

The drive felt longer than it should've. Blake kept the music up loud so he didn't have to talk to her. Part of him felt guilty for keeping her at arm's length, but his friendship with Lukas wasn't worth this. Though he had missed her. She'd become a good friend.

About a half-hour before they arrived, Paige turned down the music. "Can we go back to the way things were before I came on to you?" she asked.

He swallowed. Paige was nothing if not blunt, which was one of the things he loved about her. "I guess. Why?"

She threw up her hands. "Why? Because I liked being your friend. I was enjoying the summer, and then I had to go and make it all awkward. I'm sorry. I just want things to be easy between us again. She dropped her hands into her lap and stared at them. Blake reached over and grabbed one, giving it a squeeze.

"Sure. I missed hanging out with you too."

The touch was too much though, and so he let go. She visibly relaxed and started to chatter. This was what he'd missed.

∼

"The apartment I was going to put you in had plumbing issues yesterday, and my plumber has the flu. I've checked around, and every single room on the island is booked." Lukas ground his teeth, frustration marring his features.

Blake clapped him on the shoulder. There were worse problems they could have. "Dude, don't worry about it. I'll just crash on your couch."

Paige stood between them. "Don't be stupid, Lukas. Mom and Dad have an extra guest room. Blake can sleep there."

"You know Mom's not been feeling well. I don't want to put this on her." He chewed on his lip as if he were contemplating the solution.

"And you know she loves company. I'll make sure Blake behaves."

She nudged Blake and winked at him. Lukas gave him a questioning look, but didn't say anything. "If you're sure. I'm still not certain mom needs the company."

"Of course I'm sure. Call us a buggy, and we'll drop our bags and come back to your place for the party."

Blake absolutely did not want Lukas thinking there was anything going on.

"Maybe I should just crash on your couch." Blake rubbed at his eyes. This was exhausting.

Paige shook her head. "No way. If Mom finds out that she had a perfectly good bed and we made you sleep on the couch, both Lukas and I will be in the doghouse."

Paige pulled out a cell phone and stepped away.

"How are things going?" Lukas asked, eyes trained on Paige.

Blake shrugged. "It's a little boring out there, but that's just what I needed this summer." He didn't want Lukas to think he'd been enjoying his time with Paige.

"And Paige?"

"What about her?" He averted his eyes and landed right on Paige's backside and he flicked his eyes up and met Tess's cheeky grin. Lukas would see right through him.

"She's not driving you nuts?" Lukas asked with a chuckle.

"No, she's great actually." He tried to hide his grin, but he couldn't.

Lukas crossed his arms and glared at him. "Just how great exactly?"

"Relax. I'm just saying she's easy to live with. She does her thing, and I do mine. I make sure the house is locked up at night, and we go into town a few times a week."

Lukas relaxed. "Okay. I really do appreciate you doing this."

"It's no problem. Really. I have enjoyed the space to think about what I want to do with the rest of my life. I like it up there. I might find a quiet place like that and open up my own botany lab."

"You should talk to Adam. I imagine he'd want to invest in it."

Blake chuckled. "I imagine he would. I've made him a lot of money." Anytime he had an idea, Adam always fronted the money. Blake had millions, but it was still never enough to front the kinds of research needed to create new pharmaceuticals.

Lukas smacked him on the shoulder. "Second thought, maybe you should let us invest this time instead of him."

The buggy pulled up, and Paige waved him over.

"Duty calls. We'll drop off our things and make nice with your parents for a few."

She grinned at him as he climbed up into the buggy. "Looks like I'll be sleeping through the night here as well. I really didn't want to wake up screaming in the middle of the night at my parents' house."

Blake tugged at his collar. "I'm not sleeping with you at your parents' house."

Her face fell. "Why not?"

"Can you imagine the fallout if they saw me sneaking out in the morning?"

She gave him a sidelong glance. "That won't be a problem."

"Why not?"

"Because the guest room shares a bathroom with my room. It's a jack n jill."

Blake nodded. That was better, but he still wasn't sure he'd be getting any sleep. He would worry all night about whether or not the door to the room was actually locked.

They chatted with her parents for a bit, but Paige made an excuse to leave and then suggested riding bikes back.

They headed out into the garage, and Paige flicked on a light. There was a snowmobile and a handful of bikes. Most of them had flat tires.

"Your parents don't bike much, huh?" He thought everyone biked on the island.

"Nah. They have a buggy driver that they use. I don't see a pump either. Oh wait, this bike is good." She hauled out a tandem bike.

Blake frowned. "You know, everyone will assume we're together." He couldn't let anyone think that.

She rolled her eyes. "So let them."

She seemed a lot more comfortable with Lukas thinking things than he did. "I thought we were moving past the awkwardness."

"I'm just saying. It doesn't matter what anyone else thinks. We'll reassure Lukas that nothing is going on, and we'll be fine."

They wheeled the bike out onto the drive, and Paige climbed on the back seat. He waved to her parents and climbed on the front. He was certain that all of his friends were about to give him massive crap about this.

Tandem bikes were beyond cheezy.

He just hoped that Lukas wouldn't read too much into it.

## CHAPTER 25

Paige and Blake caught a buggy to the Pink Pony together with Tess and Lukas. No one but Lukas saw them on the tandem bike and if Paige was being honest with herself, she wanted Lukas to think that.

Their group filled the restaurant's entire patio. Tables were pushed together, and all the guys sat at one and the women at another.

Paige followed a waddling Tess to the group of women. Nerves danced in her belly. She wasn't good with groups of women even before Emery died. She wanted to follow Blake to his table, but that would not only be weird, but also look suspicious to Lukas. Maybe she should. Then again that might just make things weird again.

For some reason Blake had become her security blanket, and she wasn't sure how she felt about that.

"Oh my goodness, woman, you look like you are

about ready to pop," a petite brunette said. "Just like the first time we met."

Tess groaned and sank onto her chair, and Paige took the seat next to her.

"How did we get away with not seeing you pregnant?" Tess asked.

The woman just grinned and winked. "Who's this?"

"Oh, sorry. My manners were lost in your rudeness." Tess grinned. "This is Paige, Lukas's sister."

"I'm Bethany. I'm married to Jaime and have a stepson and a three-year-old daughter," she said. Then she pointed around the table. "That's Anna. She's Hayden's wife. They have two-year-old twins."

"We've met," Anna said. And they had, briefly. But Anna had always been a little chilly around her. She suspected it had to do with her history with Hayden, but that was minor.

"Okaaay," Bethany said. "Moving on. There's Liz. She and Adam don't have any kids yet, but she owns like three auto shops. Someday she's gonna be richer than all of us, except her hubby." Liz blushed but didn't respond. "And Mia joined our ranks last year. They're expecting, but obviously not as soon as Tess." Bethany looked around the table, and her eyes landed on an empty chair. "Where's Jessica?"

"Probably puking her guts up. Pregnancy hasn't been nice to her," Tess said.

Bethany gaped at her, and Anna giggled. "Wait, Jessica's pregnant?" Liz asked.

"Why is that so funny?" Paige asked.

"Because Jessica and Conner have been together the longest, but they still aren't married and swore they weren't having any kids. They had dogs and live in Dubai."

Paige raised her eyebrows but didn't say anything. She wondered what other things she'd learn about this group before the weekend was over.

Lunch was fun. She liked getting to know the women, and Bethany was quickly becoming her favorite. After eating, they wandered the shops.

"Oooh, we should get our tarot cards read." Anna pointed to a tiny shop tucked in between a few others. This was new, and so Paige hadn't seen it before. When she was growing up, there was no psychic on the island.

"I'll pass," Tess said and nearly everyone else agreed with her.

"I'm down," Paige said and stepped toward the shop. Anna stiffened but didn't say anything else. She and Anna ducked into the tiny space where someone was already getting their cards read.

They waited, and Anna stood by with her arms crossed. Paige didn't like this tension between the two of them. She thought about all the things she'd learned about the girls since she'd arrived.

"What's it like raising twins?" Paige asked.

"Busy." She hesitated like she wanted to say something else but didn't. If Anna gave her the cold shoulder all weekend, then this wouldn't be any fun.

"Have I done something to upset you?" Paige asked.

Anna pursed her lips. "No. Not really. It's just Hayden rarely talks about women he dated in the past, but he talks about you a lot."

"Hayden and I never dated."

"That's not because he didn't want to. Plus, he kissed you."

Paige snorted. "Yeah, when were like fifteen."

Anna picked at her nails and still wouldn't meet her eyes. "Look, it's just you were the one Hayden wishes he had dated, but didn't because of Lukas. He's never said it directly, but I know he wonders what if he had."

This was news to her. At some point she'd had a crush on him too, but that was high school. Paige shook her head. "He's like a brother to me and that kiss was years ago when we were stupid kids. He probably had a crush on me because there were a total of four girls on the island our age. I had a crush on him too, but that was a long time ago. And it doesn't even matter. I've only been around you and Hayden a few times and when we are all together, he never even looks at me. His eyes are always on you."

Anna chewed on her bottom lip. "Okay. I'm sorry I'm being all jealous. I'll work on that."

"You don't have to apologize. If you don't want to talk to me, I can hang out with the rest of the girls. We don't have to be friends." But she really hoped she didn't. She wanted all these women to like her.

Anna nudged her. "Nah, we gotta stick together now. No one else will get their cards read. I bet they tell us we'll become the best of friends."

∼

THE REST of the afternoon passed quickly, and Paige couldn't remember ever having more fun with a group of women. They all got ice cream and sat at picnic tables in the park while they waited for the guys to come back from wherever they'd disappeared to.

Bethany nudged her. "You know, we've had a lot of

fun with you around. Maybe we should make your presence permanent."

"What do you mean?"

"It means, there are still single men in our group. You could fix that," Anna said with a giggle.

Paige blushed, but didn't respond. Lukas would never let it happen.

"Let's see who could we hook her up with?" Liz mused, tapping her lips. "Seth is still too immature for a real relationship, and David too serious. Grayson would work."

Tess snorted. "You know Blake's been staying at her place this summer."

Anna almost dropped her ice cream. "What? No way. You and Blake? How did I not know about this?"

"No, it's not like that. He needed a place to stay, and I needed some help around the house. Lukas thought it would be a good idea. It's worked out well. I enjoy his company, but we're just friends."

"Oh my word. That explains lunch. He couldn't keep his eyes off of you. I thought that was weird. I never thought he'd give up on the idea of going back to Debbie," Anna said.

"Yeah, he turned up at our place a couple of months ago, completely heartbroken," Mia said.

Yeah. Because of Debbie. "I'm telling you we're just friends."

A dog ran up and leaped on the bench of the picnic table. Mia grabbed her collar. "Sera, no. Get down."

Paige swiveled in her seat. The guys were all heading their way, dogs in hand, except Sera, who had somehow escaped.

Jessica waved her hand at Blake. "You're telling me that you aren't attracted to that."

Anna snorted. "He's the best guy I know. You should at least try. All of us would love to see him settled and happy."

This was all too much for Paige. It was one thing for her to be nursing a massive crush on Blake. It was quite another for all of them to be in on it. Jessica crossed her arms. "As long as it's not with Debbie."

"Amen, sister," Anna said.

She wanted to ask more about Debbie. Blake had told her the story, but she'd bet her house that he left things out that these women knew, but before anyone could say anything else, tan and brown noses were sticking themselves into the bowls of ice cream.

Blake stood on the other side with Hayden and Anna, but his eyes were on her.

## CHAPTER 26

Blake knew he was being obvious. But damn if he couldn't keep his eyes off of Paige. Not to mention that every second he was away from her, he wondered what she was doing.

He didn't really care what Lukas thought anymore. After this trip, he was going to tell Paige how he felt and then let the chips fall where they may. He had to stay away now though because he didn't want to cause a fight during their trip.

He fell to the back of the crowd as they hiked up to Fort Mackinac and he kept Tria from entangling with the rest of the dogs.

Anna tucked her arm in his. "How are you doing?"

"Fine."

"Are you sure? Because you didn't tell me about Debbie. I've called you three times and you haven't answered a single one. Let alone called me back. You're living only a few hours from me, and you didn't bother to invite me up to see you."

She pouted.

"I'm sorry. I just...it was too much. You and Hayden are so happy and the twins. I just didn't want to bring you down. I'd already done that to both Tristan and Mia and Lukas and Tess."

"You're one of my best friends."

He squeezed her hand with his arm. "I know. That's probably why I didn't tell you. Because you would've seen right through me and made me talk about it all."

"Probably. I suppose I can forgive you. But only if you dish on what's going on with you and Paige."

He swallowed. This was the truth of why he didn't call Anna. She would've driven out to see them and would've known exactly what was going on. "Nothing."

"I'm calling B.S." She grinned.

He jerked his eyes away from Paige's backside. "Okay, maybe I like her a little."

"A little? Hmm. We'll see about that. The rest of us like her a lot, and we're trying to decide who to set her up with. Seth, Grayson, or David. What do you think? I'm thinking Grayson because David is too serious, and Seth is too immature."

Blake saw red. The thought of Paige with any one of them made him want to march up to her and claim her as his. He punched a fist into his hand without thinking. He wasn't sure what to do with his inner caveman. He'd never even knew it existed before now.

He tried to keep his composure, but Anna was already laughing. "I see how it is. What's stopping you?"

"Isn't it obvious?" Man, he was a sucker. She knew just how to get to him. "Lukas."

"I wouldn't let him stand in the way of your happiness. He'll get over it. Lukas has Tess, what's wrong with you having Paige?"

"If things don't work out with Paige, then what? It could destroy our friendship." These guys were his family. He couldn't risk that.

Anna sighed. "I guess that's something to think about. But you and Paige ought to at least entertain the idea. I think she really likes you, and you like her."

"Maybe, but not here. If we do, it will be after we head home, and we'll keep it on the down-low until we figure out otherwise." Oh geesh. He really did have it bad. It was her home, not his, but he'd started thinking of it that way.

"That seems reasonable, but you might want to make sure Seth doesn't make a move first." She motioned to the side.

Blake jerked his head up. Sure enough, Seth was walking next to Paige. A little close for Blake's comfort.

Once again, he saw red.

He stepped forward to interfere, but Anna held him back with a nod to Lukas, who was already marching their way.

Blake was too far away to hear anything, but Lukas wiggled his way in between the two of them.

At first Blake was pleased, but then he realized that Lukas would do the same thing to the both of them.

Blake didn't stand a chance.

## CHAPTER 27

Paige hadn't realized how much she missed being part of the living. She was having so much fun with all of Lukas's friends. Every single one had made her feel welcome. She'd been fairly social before Emery died, but she couldn't bring herself to go out anymore. This was good for her.

Blake kept his distance, but Paige knew that was because he didn't want Lukas to suspect anything. And she saw his point. Every time Seth or Grayson tried to talk to her, Lukas was right there, interrupting. He didn't do it when it was one of the girls or the married men—like Hayden or Jamie. Just the single guys. It was annoying, but she understood why he did it.

She knew he was just being protective. It was something he'd never been before, but after he found out what happened with Emery, he became an overbearing big brother.

A fire roared on the beach in Lukas's backyard. The kids were all inside asleep under the watchful eye of

Estelle, and the dogs were either napping under trees or chasing each other.

Several mosquito lanterns were lit and gave the whole atmosphere a romantic summer night vibe.

Paige sat in a chair by herself and watched Blake—she couldn't help herself. He stood talking with Adam and Conner. All three men had beers in hand and were laughing.

Jamie and Bethany sat by the fire, their heads together. Earlier today, Jamie had chatted with Paige about art. She pulled out her phone to google him. She found him easily and scrolled through the photographs he'd taken. He was really good. She spotted Bethany in a few of them, but nothing of his kids.

Something knocked her chair, and she jerked her head up. Blake had hauled a chair next to her and collapsed into it.

"This is the first time I've caught you alone all day." He handed her a beer.

"I know. It's been nice. I've enjoyed getting to know the girls. They are all really sweet."

"I saw you talking to Seth as well." His voice came out in a growl.

"Are you jealous?" She'd seen the way he reacted to the UPS guy. He definitely had a jealous streak. She knew it was silly, but she liked it.

He shrugged. "Maybe."

"Well, apparently he doesn't value his friendship with Lukas as much as you do." She had to force herself not to smile when she said it.

He chuckled. "Maybe not, but I saw Lukas butt in."

"Well, I didn't mind. I'm not all that interested in Seth."

She took a risk and laid her hand on his knee. She expected him to pull away, but instead he scooted closer and flung his arm across the back of her chair.

"Good thing it's dark, and Lukas can't really see us."

Holy flip. He wasn't rebuffing her.

She quickly found Lukas across the way. "He's distracted with Tess."

Blake's fingers brushed her shoulder. "That too."

"I always envied their relationship. Even before Emery died, I saw how happy and relaxed they were with each other. I want that." Her marriage with Emery was anything but happy. She didn't like thinking about it though.

"Me too."

"Do you think that maybe eventually you and Debbie will find your happiness?" She was testing him. She wanted to see if Debbie was really someone she had to worry about.

Blake choked on his beer. "No. I don't. Debbie is not someone I was ever relaxed around. I'm actually starting to realize that what she and I had was not healthy. If we'd managed to stay together, it wouldn't have lasted, and it wouldn't have been happy."

"Why now?" She was fishing. But this was the first time she'd ever got him talking about Debbie, and she wanted to know where she stood with him. They were on the verge of something, and she wasn't about to let it slip away.

"I found peace in my soul. Never before have I had that. I don't want the chaos that Debbie brings."

She swallowed and prepared herself to ask the question she really wanted to know the answer to—*how do I fit in,* but before she could, Liz waved a bag of marshmallows in the air.

"S'more time!" she yelled.

Blake chuckled and removed his arm from the back of Paige's chair, the moment ruined. "How do you like your marshmallows? Burned or golden brown."

He stood, and she blinked up at him, shocked at how quickly things had changed.

"Black of course."

He gaped at her. "Black? You're a monster."

"Monster? That's rich coming from a man who eats his bacon extra crispy."

She followed him to the fire, arguing the whole way about how to cook a marshmallow, and wondered if they'd ever talk about their feelings.

## CHAPTER 28

*B*lake brushed his teeth. Today had been a good day, but he worried about how things would go tonight. Even though he and Paige were sparking, he still wasn't ready to go all-in with her.

He needed to talk to Lukas, and he'd tried three times, but he couldn't bring himself to do it. Especially after Lukas grumbled for hours about Seth not respecting the brotherhood.

He would not risk his friendship for Paige.

Yet here they were, at her parents' house, getting ready to sleep in the same bed. He was so in for it. He had left her downstairs talking to her parents and planned on being in bed before she came up.

But just as he was yanking his shirt over his head, she knocked on the door to his room from the jack in jill bathroom.

"Come in," he called.

She poked her head in, her hair, finally out of its

ponytail, spilling in waves around her face. His fingers itched to dig into it and pull her face close to his.

He sat on his hands.

"You ready for bed?" she asked, her face hopeful.

"I am, but I think I'll sleep in here tonight."

She pouted, her bottom lip inviting him in. He closed his eyes for a moment and ran a hand along his face. She sat next to him and placed a hand on his thigh.

"Please. I can't risk waking up screaming here. After Emery died, they all treated me like I was going to break. I got so tired of people walking on eggshells around me. I managed to convince everyone I was fine and I don't want that to change now. My mom and dad don't need to be worrying about me."

"Paige, if I sleep with you here, I won't be able to keep my hands off of you."

"Is that really a bad thing?" She wiggled her eyebrows at him.

He stood up and paced in front of her. He couldn't deny how he felt about her. Not now, and he didn't know how much longer he'd be able to resist her.

"Yes. It is. For one thing, your parents are down the hall. And for another, I saw how Lukas reacted to Seth. He won't allow this to happen."

She stood and placed her hands on his stomach, causing all sorts of unwanted emotions. But he didn't pull away from her.

"We'll deal with Lukas later. What's different about the bed in here or at home?"

He waved his hand toward the bed. "That's half the size of your bed at home."

Her lips twitched. "You're exaggerating."

"Not really." It was a double bed, but still.

"We get tangled up in my big bed at home. We just won't fight it here."

He stepped around her and yanked a blanket off his bed. "Fine. But Tria is sleeping between us."

Paige clapped her hands. "Of course Tria can sleep between us."

But Blake knew that wouldn't last. Tria didn't like being trapped between two people and would end up at their feet.

## CHAPTER 29

Paige sat on Hayden's boat in a bikini, her face pointed up to the sun. She'd managed to find a quiet corner, which was what she needed right now. Everyone else was in the water, splashing and carrying on, but Paige craved alone time to think.

At least three times last night she swore Blake was going to kiss her. But he didn't, and she wasn't brave enough to make the first move herself. They had spent most of the night with her back pressed against his front and his strong arm holding her tight, but this morning he acted like nothing had changed between them, and since they'd been on the boat, he'd basically ignored her.

She was so tired of this.

The ladder behind her creaked, and she jerked her head around. Jessica came up, her wet hair trailing down the towel wrapped around her back.

"Can I lay out with you?" she asked.

"Sure."

Jessica laid out her towel next to Paige and nudged

her with her shoulder. "So. Spill. What's going on with you and Blake."

"I have no idea what you are talking about."

"Oh, come on. He won't look at you, and you won't look at him. Something happened."

Paige hadn't realized she'd been so obvious. "It's nothing more than usual. He knows how I feel about him, and he feels the same, but he won't do anything because of Lukas. I'm getting a little irritated actually."

Jessica nodded. "I see. You know, I was there when Debbie broke his heart."

"In Japan?"

"No. In Prague. Where he was going to propose. She crushed him. I really hope you're in this for the long run. I don't want to see him hurt again."

"Got it. If Blake proposes, the answer is yes." She grinned to show she was joking just a little, but at this point, she might just say yes if he did propose.

Jessica chuckled. "I knew there was a reason I liked you. I think you will become one of us after all."

## CHAPTER 30

Blake sat on the opposite side of the table from Paige, who somehow managed to get stuck between Grayson and Seth. She wore only her bikini top and a sarong wrapped around her waist, and Seth's wandering eyes bugged the hell out of Blake. Anna was on the other side of Seth and he wasn't staring at her breasts.

He kicked his leg out and got Seth right in the shin.

Seth jerked his head around. "Ow, dude, I didn't think you were Lukas."

"I'm not," Blake growled. "But I am her bodyguard this summer, and that includes keeping creeps like you away from her." Seth wasn't really a creep, but he did like his women.

Paige leaned into Seth, putting a hand on his arm. "I'm free to date whoever I want, and I can be the judge of what's creepy or not."

"He was staring at your boobs." Blake shouldn't have said anything, but he couldn't help himself.

She puffed her chest out. "I can't really blame him. They are nice looking, aren't they?" Blake nearly choked on his beer.

Seth snorted. "I don't know what you two have going on, but I'm not getting between that." He gently pushed Paige's hand off his arm. "No offense, but I only go for single girls."

"I'm single," Paige protested, giving Blake a glare. He knew what she was doing and he wasn't going to take the bait.

"Nope. You're not. I'm not an idiot. You two are sleeping together. I don't care what you tell Lukas." He grinned at both of them and put some distance between himself and Paige.

Anna raised her eyebrows at Blake. "Told you it was obvious."

"We're not sleeping together," Paige said. Which was a lie...sort of. But Blake wasn't about to correct her.

"Why not?" Seth asked.

Both Blake and Paige flicked their eyes toward Lukas, who sat on the opposite end of the table.

Seth snorted. "Dude, grow a pair and just tell him."

"It's not that simple," Blake said. He shoved his hands into his pockets and glowered at the ground. "What if I break her heart and then he never speaks to me again."

"Hello, I'm right here." Paige waved a hand. "I don't need you two Neanderthals determining my fate. But Blake, he's right. I'm tired of not getting what I want because you are scared of Lukas. I'd rather have you break my heart than always wonder what could've been."

"I like this girl, Blake. We should keep her around." Seth grinned.

Paige nodded politely. "Thank you, Seth. If Blake doesn't get his act together, maybe I'll be going home with you instead."

She smirked at Blake, and he held back his retort. She'd gotten to him, but he wouldn't give her the satisfaction of knowing it.

∼

AFTER THEY ALL watched the fireworks together Paige and Blake headed back to Paige's parents' place. Paige climbed into bed, and Blake tried not to stare. Every day it was getting harder and harder to resist her. It was warmer here in Mackinac and Paige's pajamas barely covered her.

"What's with the sunrise thing?" she asked.

"Oh, it's a tradition. Every trip we watch the sunrise together the last morning. It started several years ago when Hayden had an eight a.m. flight. We all got up to see him off, and a tradition was born. Now everyone basically heads home right afterward."

"Well, don't forget to set your alarm."

Oh, she wasn't getting away with that. "Me? You have to go too."

He climbed in under his own blanket but stayed on his side of the bed.

"No, I don't. It's your stupid tradition." He didn't know how she couldn't see that she was part of their group. They'd all embraced her.

"You're one of us now. You have to come with." He didn't know how but he had every intention of making sure she was at the next fourth of July as well. He couldn't imagine them without her.

She patted the sheets for her phone. "You might have to carry me out of here. It's been a long couple of days."

He gave her a grin, not able to help himself. "I won't mind."

She swatted his arm. "I think I left my phone downstairs. I'll grab it."

Blake's head hit the pillow, and he must've been more tired than he thought because he was out before she got back.

∼

"WHAT THE HELL?"

Lights blinded Blake as he tried to orient himself. Paige jerked up off his chest and out of his arms. Lukas towered over the both of them.

Blake scrambled out of bed and was acutely aware that he was only wearing boxers. "This isn't what it looks like."

"It looks like you are in bed with my sister. I don't know how that can look any different."

"Oh, grow up, Lukas," Paige shouted. That was not helpful.

"Grow up? Excuse me. I left my grown-up friend to take care of my grown-up sister and not screw her. Looks like I'm the only grown-up here who can control myself. But I'm done being a grown-up."

If Blake had been more awake, he would've seen it coming, but he wasn't, so when Lukas's fist connected with his nose, his head snapped back.

He didn't bother hitting back. He'd deserved it.

"Lukas!" Paige shouted. But he stormed from the room. Blake tried running after him, but Paige stopped him. "You're bleeding and not dressed. Let me help you clean up and then we can go after him."

Blake held a hand up to his nose. "Not we. Me. I'm the one he's mad at, not you."

Paige didn't argue, for which Blake was grateful for and helped him clean his face. His nose throbbed with the pain.

"I don't think it's broken, but you'll definitely have a black eye."

That was a small price to pay. He pulled on a pair of shorts and tugged a t-shirt over his head, avoiding any contact with his face.

He'd planned on just packing up their stuff before they left for the sunrise, but depending on how long it took with Lukas, they could miss the first ferry. "Can you pack my stuff up? We'll head home after I'm done with him."

"What if he tries to stop you from taking me home?"

"We're adults, remember? We don't need his permission. But I would like his blessing." It was time to stop playing games with Paige. He was ready to take this to the next level.

She wouldn't look him in the eye. "And if he doesn't give it?"

"He knows now. Blessing or not, I'm done trying to pretend I don't have feelings for you."

He left before her response and jogged to Lukas's house, unsure if he was really there or not, but it was his best starting point. They were supposed to ride to the beach for the sunrise with Lukas and Tess, but he doubted Lukas headed there after their fight.

He knocked, and Tess answered the door, Jack hiding behind her legs.

"Is he here?" he asked.

Tess nodded. "Collapsed on the couch. He told me to not let you in if you showed up, but I'm on your side." She reached over and squeezed his arm. "Come on. Let's see if we can convince him that you and Paige belong together."

Lukas didn't open his eyes when Blake and Tess entered the room. Blake sat on the recliner across from the couch, and Tess sat next to Lukas. Jack crawled up into Lukas's lap. Maybe that would prevent him from calling Blake any colorful names.

"Listen, Paige and I haven't had sex, and we've only kissed once in the grocery store, and that was just to prove a point to an obnoxious pair of women."

Lukas glared at him. "Bull. I found you in bed with her."

"Okay. We've been sleeping in the same bed together for a few weeks now. Paige has nightmares. The first week I was there, she woke up screaming every night, and I went to her room and helped her calm down. You asked me to protect her, and that's what I'm doing. After talking more about it, we don't think she saw anyone the night she called the sheriff. That was all part of her nightmares. The accident has left scars that no one can see. One night we watched a movie together and fell asleep. That was the first night since the accident that she didn't have a nightmare. And she hasn't had one since."

Lukas clenched his fists. Blake wasn't sure he believed him.

"That was very sweet of you," Tess said. "Paige didn't tell me about that."

Lukas opened and closed his fists. "Paige is fragile."

"She's stronger than you think," Blake said. And she was. Sure, she was having trouble now, but she'd overcome huge obstacles.

"And that's why you're sleeping with her every night?" Lukas growled.

"You know," Tess began. "We like Paige, like all the wives. I do too, but you already knew that. She's a good addition to our group."

Lukas didn't respond right away.

"I haven't seen her laugh like she has this trip in a long time," Lukas said, staring off into space.

"Right? You know what's changed?" Tess asked, waving her hands toward Blake.

Lukas eyed him. "Tess, you don't think that the change is because of Blake?"

"I do. Blake has does his best to respect you, but Paige wants more. Blake is the one holding out."

"Did she tell you that?"

"Yes. And if you weren't blind, you'd see how she looks at him. She and Blake would make an adorable couple."

"Tess," Lukas warned.

"What? You don't think so?" she huffed.

Blake was grateful he could just sit back and listen. Tess was doing his dirty work for him, and he had no problem letting her.

"She's my sister."

"Would you rather see her with some guy she meets in a few years that you don't know and that you're not sure you could trust? I'd much rather see her with Blake."

Blake gripped the arms of the chair a little harder than necessary. The thought of some other guy putting his hands on her caused jealousy to rise in his chest. But he had no right to that jealousy. Not yet, anyway.

"No. I don't want to see her with anyone," Lukas said his fist clenched and staring at the fireplace.

"You want her to be unhappy?" Tess asked, her voice cracking. "That's cruel."

He jerked his head around, his face a mess of emotion. "That's not what I meant. I just…I just…don't want to see her hurt again. What happened with Emery broke her."

"He died in a car accident."

"That's not what I'm talking about."

Tess swallowed. They knew. Blake had assumed Paige hadn't told anyone about that.

"I'm not going to cheat on her and you know it," Blake said.

Lukas met his eyes. "She told you."

Blake nodded.

Tess wrapped an arm around Lukas's waist and leaned into him. "Blake's a good guy, right? You know he wouldn't hurt her. Wouldn't you rather she date him than some other schmuck that might break her heart?"

Lukas eyed Blake, but Blake didn't say a word. He wanted to know what Lukas was about to say.

"You have a point."

"So, will you stay out of the way and let them figure things out themselves?"

Lukas stared at him. "You and Paige are adults. I trust you far more than anyone else. I won't stand in your way or get angry, but I reserve the right to punch you in the nose again if you hurt her." His jaw was set. Lukas didn't like this, but Blake would take it.

"Fair enough. Thank you."

Blake wasn't sure what would happen now, but he was ready to fall.

## CHAPTER 31

Paige gathered her things and texted Blake that she'd meet him at the ferry. They were all planning on leaving after the sunrise, but now she'd have to get their things together for the both of them. She had no idea what her parents had heard and had no interest in finding out their thoughts. So she packed both her and Blake's things. By the time she left, they weren't even out of their room. She left a note telling them that she loved them and was out the door before seven.

She tipped the carriage driver generously and got out to join Jessica and Conner, who were waiting for the ferry.

"Missed you guys at the sunrise." Jessica leaned into Connor. They were all supposed to see the sunrise before they left, but obviously her morning had gone awry.

"Yeah, my alarm didn't go off." If only she'd set her alarm, none of this would've happened.

"Blake wasn't there either."

"He's talking to Lukas." She hoped that it was going well. She'd never seen Lukas so angry.

Jessica raised her eyebrows. "About?"

Paige gave a noncommittal shrug. She was saved by Jamie and his family's arrival and Tristan and Mia. No one else asked why she wasn't there though Tristan asked where Blake was. Jessica answered for Paige.

Just as the ferry was pulling up, Blake showed up, his eyes now both black.

Tristan whistled. "Dude, what happened to your face?"

"I don't want to talk about it," he growled.

Jessica snickered. "I bet I know." But Blake glared at her.

He took his own bag and sat with Jamie and his family. Paige found her own seat, but Jessica followed.

Paige's phone buzzed. It was a message from Tess.

*Lukas gave his blessing. In three days, I want details.*

Paige's face flushed, and Jessica didn't miss it. "What happened?" she asked.

Paige just showed her the phone, and she squeed. "So why is he sitting back there?"

"I don't know." A bad feeling settled in her gut. This didn't make sense. If Lukas said he was okay with things, Blake had no reason to ignore her.

"So. Did Lukas punch him?"

"Yeah."

Twice, it appeared.

"For just telling him he had feelings for you?" She wasn't sure how Blake felt about her. She knew he kinda liked her, but she wasn't certain how far it went.

Because instead of him coming to the ferry and kissing her senseless, he was ignoring her.

Paige swallowed. She didn't know how to explain this, because while they were sleeping together, they weren't really romantically involved. It'd be easier to just say they were grown adults having sex.

"Jessica, leave the poor girl alone," Conner said with a sheepish grin.

"It's okay. It's a long story. Blake and I share a bed but we're not *sleeping* together. I have some PTSD from the accident and Blake keeps my nightmares away. Lukas found him in bed with me."

Jessica squeed again and clapped her hands. "I bet he keeps those nightmares away. I'm with Tess. I'll set up a group text with all of the wives, and you are totally giving us deets in a few days."

Paige flushed.

She just hoped she'd have deets to share.

~

PAIGE WAS a little irked by the time they got back to the mainland and on the road home. Blake hadn't been behaving any differently toward her, but Tess had assured Paige that Lukas gave Blake his blessing. That meant everything should be okay, but maybe he was just using Lukas as an excuse, and he really wasn't interested in her at all.

Now she felt dumb and a little hurt. Jessica and the others would be messaging her in a few days and she'd have nothing to share. Not only that, she'd really been looking forward to pursuing this thing with Blake.

"You okay?" Blake asked. "You've been quiet this morning."

"Yeah. I'm fine. I had a really nice time this weekend. The girls were all so nice."

"I didn't think you liked people all that much, but you seemed to get along with them."

Paige let out a sigh. "I didn't use to be like that. After Emery died, I don't know. It broke me a little."

"You seem to be coming back into yourself."

"I am. It feels nice." She didn't feel all that nice at the moment, but overall she'd been feeling better.

He didn't say anything for a second. "You know, Tess said that they wanted to make you one of them."

Paige hesitated a moment before saying anything. She wanted to make sure she understood loud and clear what he was saying because she didn't want there to be any more confusion. "And how did she propose that they do that?"

"Well, you'd have to marry one of us. We're going fast though. Only four left."

She forced a laugh. He was still being vague. "I thought we agreed not to make this awkward anymore."

"What do you mean?"

"Well, there's only one of the four that I'm even remotely interested in, and you made it very clear that that wasn't happening. So why bring it up now?"

"I never said I wasn't interested in you."

"So are you?"

He let out a breath. "Yeah. I am."

She thought for a moment. She didn't want him getting all freaked out by all of this. "I've never had a summer fling before. This should be fun."

Blake gripped the steering wheel and he frowned.

"I'm not really a summer fling kind of guy. I've told you this before. If that's what you want, maybe we should just stay friends."

"So what do you want?" She wanted him to say it.

"If we're going to do this, I'm going all-in."

Paige sat there stunned for a moment. She hadn't expected such a declaration. She just kinda figured they'd kiss at some point, and things would go from there.

"What do you mean, you're all-in?"

"It means that I have no intention of leaving after the summer is over. It means that I can finally sleep naked again. It means that if you want to make it official and become one of the wives, I'm down."

"Did you just propose to me?" she squeaked.

He laughed. "Oh no. That doesn't count. I can do better than that."

## CHAPTER 32

*B*lake hadn't meant for everything to come out like that. He'd been thinking about how to tell her all the way home, and he'd planned on making a nice dinner and then telling her how he felt.

But after she'd told him how she felt about him, he couldn't help himself.

"So what about you? Are you all-in?" he asked.

"I thought I'd made that clear."

"No, you just told me you wanted my body, not necessarily everything that goes with it."

She smacked him on the shoulder. "I did not."

"Ow. Yes, you did." He chuckled. He wasn't sure how this had happened. But living together could do that to people. They'd grown comfortable with one another, and life was easy with her. He enjoyed it.

"I want it all. But maybe a better proposal."

"You've got it. Remember that when it happens, you asked for it."

"I will."

How had this happened? They hadn't even really kissed yet—the grocery store did not count—and here they were talking about the rest of their lives together.

They both went quiet for the next several miles. He wanted to reach over and take her hand.

"What are you thinking about?" Blake asked.

"That we've gone and made this awkward again. I mean, do I hold your hand or not? When we kiss, is it going to be all weird and forced? And if you climb into bed naked tonight, I promise it's gonna be weird."

He chuckled.

"I won't. But listen, let's just let things move naturally. If we don't kiss for several days, that's fine. It'll come when it comes. Both of us are a little out of practice. It'll be fine."

"Okay."

"Okay."

~

PAIGE DISAPPEARED into her art studio the second they arrived home and hadn't emerged for a few hours. Blake took Tria for a walk, spent some time in his gym, and now he missed her. She was the presence in his life that was always around, and now she wasn't, and he had no idea why.

He knocked on the door to her studio.

"Come in," she called.

He poked his head in. She stood in the middle of the room, surrounded by various canvases and covered in paint.

"You look good," he said with a chuckle.

She stuck her tongue out at him, the only pink on

her green and blue face. "Inspiration struck, and so I ran with it."

None of the new pictures were finished, only the beginnings of her visions on each canvas, but they looked good.

"I look forward to seeing the final product. Were you planning on working the rest of the night?" He hoped the answer was no. He wanted to spend time with her.

"No. I'm about done today."

"How would you feel about picnicking down on the beach? I can pack some food up while you clean up."

"Who says I need to clean up?" She popped a hand on her hip.

"Well, if you don't, that will be one messy picnic. But I'm open to it."

She shook her head at him. "Go pack that picnic. I'll meet you in the kitchen."

## CHAPTER 33

Paige was fairly certain she still had green paint behind her ear, but she didn't care. She was in a hurry to get to Blake. She'd needed that time in her studio to regroup and figure out where everything in her world stood, but now she just wanted to be with him.

She threw on a long sundress and a sweater. Even in the middle of the summer, the nights were cool by the water. It took her longer than she'd hoped to get ready because she had to blow dry her hair. Otherwise, she would really freeze.

She put on a pair of strappy sandals and skipped down the stairs. Blake was still putting food into the basket. He looked up, and his eyes sparkled.

"You look gorgeous."

She blushed. "Thanks."

"You want to grab a blanket, and we'll head out?"

They both had their hands full as they walked down

to the beach and made small talk about the weather and the many birds that flew around them.

She spread out the blanket, and Blake dug out a bottle of wine and a couple of glasses. He handed her one and tugged her close to him. Neither said a word as they sipped their wine.

"This is beautiful," he said. The lake spread out in front of them, framed by tall pines with waves lapping up on the shore. Birds chirped in the canopy above them. Everything about the place was peaceful.

"I know. I'll miss it if I move to back to Mackinac." If Blake didn't stay with her, Lukas would find a way to make her move back.

"I like it here. I see no reason to move back."

He smiled at her, she wondered if that would be the moment when they finally kissed, but he let go of her and stepped away. Disappointment flooded her chest, but she didn't say anything.

He set his glass down and pulled out plates and other things. She sat next to him, probably closer than she would've two days ago.

"We've got grapes, strawberries, blueberries, and raspberries. I didn't know what you liked best, so I brought them all. Which would you prefer?"

"I don't care. Surprise me."

He raised his eyebrows at her. "Is that how it's going to be?"

"What do you mean? I do like them all."

"Fine. Close your eyes."

"Why?"

"Because you said you wanted to be surprised."

"Fine." She said with a grin and closed her eyes.

She could hear rustling in the basket, and then Blake shifted next to her.

"Open up," he said. She wasn't expecting this, but parted her lips a little. He pressed a raspberry into her mouth, his finger lingering on her lip. She chewed and swallowed the sweet fruit and waited. This time it was a blueberry, but instead of simply letting his finger linger, he traced her bottom lip and then her top.

She wanted to open her eyes and watch him, but that would ruin the moment. So, she kept her eyes closed and waited. The anticipation was excruciating.

"This one is my favorite," he whispered in her ear.

She waited and then felt lips press against hers. The kiss was soft and deliberate, creating a mess of desire in her body, but it was over way too fast. She blinked her eyes open and found him staring deep into her eyes.

"Did I tell you that you could open your eyes?"

"What do I get if I close them again?"

"More of my favorite," he whispered.

She quickly closed her eyes, and he chuckled. "You like that one too, huh?" he mumbled against her lips.

"Very much."

He kissed her again, just as lightly as before, but this time he didn't pull away. She wanted to fling her arms around him and pull him close and maybe rip his shirt off, but she let him lead.

His lips moved gently against hers, and she responded in kind. He parted his lips and slowly licked the edge of hers. Every movement was slow and deliberate. She'd never been kissed like this before in her life.

He brought a hand to her face and stroked her cheek, still placing light kisses on her lips with the occasional flick of the tongue. Desire burned in her stomach.

She leaned up and pressed harder into the kiss, and he wrapped an arm around her waist and pulled her onto his lap. She squeaked, and he chuckled.

She opened her eyes, and they just stared at each other for a few moments. She relished this moment with him and was so grateful he'd waited until now to kiss her because this night would be unforgettable.

"Thank you," she said.

"For what? Kissing you?"

"Yes, but also for making it memorable."

He pecked her nose. "You're welcome."

He lay back on the blanket, but she didn't climb off of him. She hovered over him, her hands on his chest. He placed his hands on her hips and moved her forward a few inches.

She leaned over him and watched his eyes for a moment. They were stormy with desire. She crushed her lips against his, much more aggressively than he had with her, but he didn't disappoint. He gripped the back of her head, and their lips and tongues moved furiously against each other.

He moved his hands down her back and held her tight against him. This was a night she'd never forget.

## CHAPTER 34

Blake tugged the blanket over Paige's shoulders. She lay across his chest, fast asleep. He hadn't meant for them to spend the night on the beach, yet here they were.

The sky was just starting to lighten, but he could still see stars for miles.

"It's cold," Paige muttered, shimmying closer to him. He didn't think that was possible.

"I know. Should we go inside? We can probably catch a few more hours of sleep."

She propped up on his chest and wiggled her eyebrows. "I'm awake now, and yes, we should definitely head inside and crawl into bed, but I have no intention of going back to sleep."

He grinned at her. "What exactly do you plan on doing?"

"Many, many nefarious things."

"Then let's go."

She stood and wrapped the blanket around her, and

he took the one they'd been laying on. Paige was far more aggressive than he'd thought she be, and it drove him mad. He wondered what other surprises she had up her sleeve.

~

PAIGE SAT on the counter watching him cook again. He liked having her there.

Her phone buzzed, and she picked it up and frowned.

"What's wrong?" he asked.

"What? Oh, nothing. It's just one of my best friends texted me about a weekend retreat."

"When is it?"

"This coming weekend. I used to go every year with my artist friends, but I haven't been since Emery died. They always invite me though and they've been bugging me for a few weeks."

"You should go."

She shook her head. "I don't think I'm ready for that."

"I think you are. Look at how far you've come this past weekend. Where is it?"

"Vegas."

"Excellent. I'll come with you, and we'll spend a couple of extra nights and make this thing official."

She laughed. "You've gotta work on your proposals."

"Damn. I guess that was another lame one. Will you say yes if the proposal is better?"

She winked at him. "I'm not answering that. You'll just have to wait and see, but I won't answer at all unless there is a ring involved and a huge to-do."

"You have high expectations."

She plucked a piece of bacon off the plate next to her. "I do."

"Yep. Those are the words I want to hear. But Vegas, seriously. You should go. It will be good for you." He wanted her to go because it would be good for her, but he would miss her.

"Are you trying to get rid of me? I thought you liked sleeping with me."

"I do, but I also think it's important for you to create some normalcy in your life. That includes doing retreats with your artist friends. But what kind of retreat happens in Vegas? It seems like the Arizona desert would be better."

She giggled. "It used to be in the Utah mountains, but as the years went on, we stopped painting and spent the whole weekend talking. So we moved the location to Vegas, and none of us bring any art supplies anymore."

"What do you do then?"

She winked. "What happens in Vegas..."

"I still think you should go."

"I do too. I haven't seen most of them since the funeral. This will be like starting over. I'm ready to do that. Well, I started with you, but you're right. I need to take the rest of my life back."

She picked up her phone and sent a quick message back.

"Will you hold down the fort while I'm gone?"

"I won't sleep as well, but yeah I will." He'd gotten used to sleeping with her in his arms. He supposed Tria would have to do.

Her eyes widened. "Oh no. You have to come with. Otherwise I won't be able to sleep."

He gave her a quick kiss. "No. This will be a good

trial. You need to prove that you can do this alone. Otherwise I'll never know if you're staying with me because you love me, or because you just want a good night's sleep."

She rolled her eyes. "Because I love you. Duh."

## CHAPTER 35

Paige stepped out of the airplane and into the dry hot air. She wondered why they did this in the summer. They should totally do it in the winter when the weather was better.

She caught a cab and took it to the timeshare that her friend Emma owned. It was right on the strip and had three bedrooms. She was still nervous about sleeping alone, but she hadn't had a nightmare since Blake started sleeping with her, and she was definitely moving on.

She grabbed a key from the front desk and took the elevator up to the twenty-first floor. Her friend had the penthouse. Which wasn't saying much for Vegas, but it was still nice. She popped the door open and was greeted by squeals.

Donna reached her first. She was the oldest of the group. She never told them her age, but Paige guessed she was in her mid-sixties. Donna squeezed Paige tightly, and the other two waited for their turn.

Naveen and Stormy dragged her to the couch and pushed a glass of champagne into her hand. They both plopped down on either side of her, and Donna took the chair across from them, her eyes sparkling.

"So," she started, "I've been tasked with asking what changed this year?"

She knew this was going to come up. These girls never pulled any punches. It was one of the things she loved about them. But she wasn't sure she was ready to share about Blake. "Who said anything changed? Maybe I was just feeling better. Grief is weird."

She dropped her eyes to her champagne glass, and Stormy squeezed her other hand. "Hon, we're sorry. We don't mean to be insensitive, but, well, you know Donna is friends with Ida, and she told her that you were living with some hunk."

"Hunk? What decade are we in? The eighties?"

Stormy cackled. "You're deflecting. There is a guy. Spill. We haven't had good romance drama among us since that year Donna spent our girls' weekend holed up in another hotel with that Casanova from Spain."

Donna flushed.

"Whatever happened with him anyway?" Paige asked.

"Stop trying to change the subject." Naveen shook her finger at Paige. "We want to hear about your man."

Paige sighed and pulled up a picture of him on her phone. "Fine. His name is Blake, and he was my bodyguard and driver for the summer. I stopped driving after…" She let her words trail off.

"That is so cliché. You fell for your bodyguard. Why did you need one anyway?" Stormy asked.

"I didn't. But I had a scare where I thought someone had been in my house, and my brother freaked out.

Turns out it was just a hallucination. But Blake is one of Lukas's friends, and he needed a place to stay for the summer since he was between jobs. Lukas volunteered him."

She held her phone out so her friends could see a picture of them together.

"Holy mother of all things hot," Stormy whispered. "You upgraded girl."

Donna smacked her on the arm.

"What? We all knew Emery was no good for Paige. I just kept waiting for the divorce. I wouldn't have wished him dead though." Her face went serious.

"It's still insensitive." Donna frowned.

"It's okay. I've made my peace with it. If he hadn't died, we would've gotten divorced. He was cheating on me." Anger mixed with guilt still raged every time she thought about it.

A collective gasp went through them all. Then Stormy giggled. "It's not funny. I'm sorry. But it's just so absurd. He cheated on you? Like he had it so good. I fully expected you to wake up one day and realize how much better you were than him. Him cheating on you just seems ridiculous."

Paige hadn't realized her friends felt that way about him, but it wasn't a good marriage. She knew that now. She also knew he wasn't a good guy. Not only was he a cheating bastard, but he was also overbearing and superficial.

"Yeah, well. I was blind."

Stormy scooted closer to her. "Enough about him. Tell us more about Mr. Muscles there."

"He's everything Emery was not. He's kind and caring. He cooks for me, and he likes my art. He never judges me for all my weird grief symptoms. He's just there. I'm absolutely in love with him. But I keep waiting for the other shoe to drop. For him to leave me or do something super douchey. I dunno. I guess I feel like I don't deserve him."

"That's ridiculous," Stormy said. "You deserve love like that more than anyone else I know."

Paige hoped Stormy was right because she didn't feel like she deserved it at all.

## CHAPTER 36

Blake was ready for Paige to come home. She'd sent him silly pictures and sappy drunk texts. They Facetimed every night so she could feel like he was sleeping with her even though he wasn't. He missed her more than he'd thought he would. This was an unfamiliar feeling for him. He never missed Debbie when they were apart. Every time they broke up, he mourned the loss of their relationship, but this longing to just have someone near was new.

He picked up the phone and dialed Lukas.

"What's up? Is Paige okay?"

"Oh, yeah. She's fine. She's in Vegas with her artist friends."

"And you didn't go with her?"

"It was a girls' weekend."

"She hasn't done one of those since Emery died." Lukas' voice dropped a little.

"I know."

"You've been good for her."

"Thanks. I've missed her while she's been gone." Blake rubbed the back of his neck. He wasn't sure how Lukas would take the next thing he asked. "So...I know your dad is probably the one I should be asking, but I thought it would be more appropriate for me to ask you instead."

"Ask me what?"

"Permission to marry Paige."

Lukas went very quiet for a few seconds. "Have you asked her yet?"

"No. Well, yeah, but not very seriously. She wants a big to-do. But I didn't want to do it without your permission." Blake didn't want to do anything that would jeopardize his friendship with Lukas so he needed this.

"Of course he'll give you it," Tess yelled from somewhere near Lukas.

Blake chuckled.

"I've only ever wanted my sister to be happy. You make her happy. So yeah, marry her."

Blake let out a breath of relief. "Thanks, man. I'm not sure what I'll do for the proposal yet, but I'll probably need your help. Is that okay?"

"Of course. But just remember we've got a baby due soon, when you're doing your planning."

Blake chatted with them a little longer and then hung up. His phone immediately rang again, and Paige's face filled his screen.

"Hey, gorgeous. I can't wait to see you."

She giggled. "Me neither. I'm getting on a plane in like ten minutes. You'll pick me up, right?"

"Sure. Is a sign at the airport a big enough to-do?" He

knew she'd say no, but this was part of the game they played.

"For what?"

"My proposal. Duh?"

She giggled. "Think bigger." An announcement played in the background. "That's me. Gotta run. See you in a few hours. Love you."

"Love you too." He hung up the phone and thought. Bigger. He had to make sure it was the biggest damn proposal Paige had ever seen. To make sure it exceeded her expectations in every way.

The phone rang again, but he didn't recognize the number.

"Mr. Turner?"

"Yes."

"I'm calling about Operation Maple Leaf. Your assistance is needed immediately. Please give me your location, and we will send a helicopter for you that will take you to the nearest airport where a jet will be waiting."

Blake sighed and gave the man his address. He regretted signing up for this project. Now there was no telling when he'd see Paige again. The last time they called, he was holed up for two weeks.

The project was the joint effort of several pharmaceutical companies. They created Operation Maple Leaf to solve their toughest problems. But it was incredibly secretive. When the helicopter arrived to pick him up, they would take his phone and only return it once they dropped him back off.

He immediately dialed Paige, but her phone was already on airplane mode and went straight to voicemail.

"Hey, baby, I'm so sorry, but I won't be here when you get home. Occasionally I get summoned for special projects in my field, and they literally just called me. I can't explain everything in a voicemail, but call Jessica when you arrive, and she'll explain what happened the last time I was summoned. I won't have my phone, and I don't know how long I'll be gone. The last few times it's been between three days and three weeks. I'll call you as soon as I can. I love you."

He raced upstairs and packed a quick bag. He put out food for Tria. Paige would be home soon and would take good care of her.

He wanted to call Lukas and ask him to come stay with Paige while he was gone, but then he heard the woosh-woosh of helicopter blades. Dammit. He had to go.

Instead he called Ida. "Can you pick up Paige from the airport? I'll text you the flight info. I have a work emergency."

"Sure thing. You gonna be okay?"

"Yeah. Tell Paige I love her."

"Will do."

He raced out to the waiting helicopter where a man in a black suit held out his hand. "Cell phone please."

Blake handed it over and hoped that he wouldn't regret this.

## CHAPTER 37

*P*aige didn't bother turning her cell phone back on. She just wanted to see Blake. The airport was small enough that he'd be waiting just on the other side of the escalators. She raced down the hall and searched for his face among the waiting family and friends, but he wasn't there. Instead, she saw Ida.

"What are you doing here?" Paige asked.

"Blake asked me to pick you up. He had some sort of work emergency."

Work emergency? She'd talked to him just before she got on the plane, and he'd said nothing of the sort. They settled into the car, and then she turned her phone on. She pressed it to her ear as she listened to the voicemail.

Three weeks! She didn't like this at all.

"You okay?" Ida asked.

"What? Yeah, I'm fine. I just thought Blake would be here is all."

Ida dropped her off at her house, and she set her bags by the door and immediately dialed Jessica.

"Hey, Paige. What's up?."

"Listen, um, Blake told me to call you. He got summoned or something, and I was on a plane, and so all he did was leave me a voicemail."

Jessica chuckled. "Yep. I remember that well. He got a call one time when he was staying with us in Dubai, and a helicopter showed up like ten minutes later. We didn't hear from him for another ten days when the helicopter dropped him back off."

"What is it?"

"I don't really know. I do know he and Debbie made up on the last trip. But Blake never talked about the work side of things."

Debbie. The ex-girlfriend. The love of his life.

"Thanks, Jessica. I guess all I can do is wait at this point, right?"

"Yeah. Sorry. You want us to come stay with you? Blake said you don't like being alone."

"I'll be okay. I have Tria."

"Okay. Well if you need anything, you call."

"I will."

Paige put down the phone and then grabbed her laptop off the counter. She pulled up Facebook and did a quick search of Blake's friends. From the looks of it, Blake hadn't been on Facebook in ages. She found Debbie easily.

She was a pretty, sophisticated blonde woman. Practically the opposite of Paige. Her page was public, so Paige could see all of her posts. The last one was posted just a few hours ago with no picture. "Going offline for work. See you suckers on the other side."

Jealousy rose up in Paige's chest. So she and Blake would be together. No. Blake wouldn't cheat on Paige.

He was one of the good guys. But everyone, including Blake, acted like Debbie was his Achilles heel. Paige wondered if Debbie still had a hold on him or if Paige had managed to break that.

Paige scoffed. She and Blake hadn't been together long enough for her to have that kind of influence. But Debbie was happily married so hopefully that would keep them all from doing anything stupid.

Paige's curiosity got the better of her, so she continued scrolling. Debbie's page was mostly pictures of herself at fancy events. She thought quite highly of herself. In all of the pictures she was alone or with girlfriends.

Debbie was one of those women who was very open about everything on her social media page: political beliefs, rants against companies she hated, and raves about her favorite restaurants. But she also posted some uncomfortable personal stuff as well. There were a handful of posts about a fight with her sister and one that called her boss out for being unfair.

She was exactly the kind of person that Paige would never be comfortable around.

Paige scrolled farther and found a post that made her freeze. There was a picture of Debbie with puffy eyes and black streaks down her cheeks.

*This has got to be the shortest marriage on record. This afternoon I went for a massage but found out it had been canceled. When I got back to my hotel room, do you know what I found? My brand spanking new husband naked in bed with the housekeeper. Who cheats on their wife during the honeymoon?*

A weight settled in her chest. Debbie wasn't happily married.

Paige clicked over to the pictures and scrolled until she found pictures of Debbie with Blake. They looked like they belonged together. Both dressed up with champagne glasses in their hands. In all of the pictures, Blake wore button-down shirts and had his hair slicked back. Here, he always wore t-shirts and shorts, and his hair was never done. But she liked messy Blake. He fit in her world.

This polished version of him did not.

She clicked off of her computer. She might as well get used to sleeping alone. Those two were made for each other. He was made for that life. Maybe he'd been living some fantasy here, and now he'd figure out what he really wanted.

He'd probably told Paige all those things about being over Debbie just so she didn't worry. He knew she didn't have a lot of relationship experience. Blake would go back to Debbie, and their shiny world and she would be stuck here, all alone.

## CHAPTER 38

Blake dropped his bag next to his bunk. As long as they were here, he wouldn't get more than a few hours of sleep at a time. This was an emergency, and they would work round the clock until it was fixed. He wasn't the first to arrive, and Debbie wasn't here yet either.

He didn't really want to see her. Debbie had a way of making everything about her, and he didn't want to deal with her drama. He hadn't realized how much it bothered him until he started dating Paige. She was so easy. He didn't know women could be like that. He'd just assumed they were all like Debbie. Or in the case of his friend's wives, hiding it around others.

"I'm getting too old for this," a voice said. Blake spun around and found Jacob standing behind him. He dropped his bag on the bunk next to Blake's.

"Yeah, you gonna retire from the team after this?" Jacob was an infectious disease specialist and the best in his field, but he was probably nearing his seventies by now.

"I could try, but they won't let me."

Blake chuckled. "Well. At least you know you'll be saving lives."

Patricia poked her head in the door. "Everyone's here. They're going to brief us now."

Blake went into the lab and spotted Debbie on the other side of the room, tapping a finger on her knee. She probably didn't know what to do with herself without her phone.

She glanced over and met his eye. She gave him one of her million-watt smiles, but it didn't affect him like it used to. He gave her a nod hello though.

Dr. Oaks walked in, and everyone quieted. Blake had been with this team for several years now, and he still didn't know Dr. Oaks's first name.

"Okay people. An Ebola-like disease has been discovered in a small town in Bolivia. So far it's contained, but it's airborne."

A collective gasp went around the room. They'd always talked about what would happen if Ebola went airborne. Two-thirds of the earth's population would be wiped out.

"What's the fatality rate?" Jacob asked.

"Eighty percent."

Blake whistled. "What do you need from us?"

Dr. Oaks's face remained serious. "We need a treatment. None of the medicines for Ebola have proven effective. You guys need to find something that will kill this son of a bitch."

Blake rubbed a hand along his face. This would not be an easy task, and he would have to work closely with

Debbie. Once Dr. Oaks ended his speech and handed out assignments, Blake headed to his usual table. Debbie was already there, poring over the reports. He wondered if she even bothered listening or just got right to work.

"Anything useful in there?"

She shook her head. He didn't want this to be awkward because they had to work together.

"Congrats on your marriage."

She jerked her head up, her face a mask of surprise.

"It's over."

"It was just like two months ago."

"He cheated on me during my honeymoon."

Ouch.

"I'm sorry." Though he was no longer in love with her, he still wanted her to be happy.

She shrugged. "It's over, and I'm okay. That just means you and I can sneak off to the bunk room when we need a break." She winked at him. So much for things not being awkward.

Paige's beautiful face flashed in his mind. "I'm seeing someone."

"So."

"So, I won't cheat on her." Debbie was never one to care for boundaries like that. He wondered how often she cheated on him.

She placed a hand on his arm and puffed her chest out. "Come on, Blake. We both knew it was only a matter of time before we got back together. This seems as good a time as any."

"No, Debbie, It's over."

Forever this time.

She bristled but didn't say anything else. If it were possible to do this job without talking to her again,

Blake would, but saving lives was more important than trying to avoid her.

~

EIGHT DAYS LATER, Blake finally emerged from his cave. A treatment was found, and they would all breathe a little easier knowing that disease wasn't about to be unleashed on the world.

He hopped on a plane and laid his head back on the headrest. Not only had he managed to help find the treatment, but he also managed to avoid Debbie's advances while there. And there were a lot. She was always touching him and giggling.

As they parted ways, she kissed him on the cheek and told him she'd see him soon. She didn't get it. But he'd been firm with her, and hopefully she wouldn't try this again.

He was going home to the love of his life.

And he couldn't wait.

## CHAPTER 39

*E*ight days was a long time.

Paige couldn't sit still. She managed to get three full works of art done, but Blake wasn't there so she couldn't deliver anything to the shop. She kept her phone next to her and checked it no less than fifty times an hour.

She just wanted to hear from him. A text would be fine, but there was nothing. She did listen to his voicemail every night before she went to bed. She woke up with nightmares again every night, but this time Blake died in her dreams, not Emery. She just needed to hear his voice or see his face.

She hated being this needy.

She took Tria out for a walk by the beach and sat and stared out at the soft waves.

Her phone buzzed, and she jerked. She grabbed it out of her pocket.

There was a notification on her Facebook page. She rolled her eyes. That wasn't what she'd been waiting for, but she opened it anyway. Blake had been tagged in a post.

It was a picture of him and Debbie, an old one. The only reason Paige knew that was because Blake's hair was much longer than it was now. In the picture, Debbie had her hand on Blake's chest, and he was staring at her like she's the only woman in the world.

Paige quickly read the post.

*The dream team has been at it again. Saving the world one cure at a time. Blakey, it was amazing working with you again and burning the midnight oil ;-). Can't wait to see you again soon. XOXO*

Paige swallowed. Her worst nightmare had come true. She should've known things with Blake with too good to be true. She stood, wiped her sweating palms on her jeans, and trudged back up to the house.

She would make it through this, but she had to take time to process this first.

And when he did show up, she wouldn't allow Blake in her house.

## CHAPTER 40

The helicopter touched down in Paige's yard, and the pilot handed him his phone.

He didn't bother to turn it on. He just jogged up to the house. He stopped dead just before he reached the door. Sitting on the front porch was his suitcases and his dog.

His heart sank.

He tried the door, but it was locked. He hauled out his own keys, and while they opened the locks, Paige had thrown the slide lock. He pounded on the door.

"Paige, I don't know what's going on, but whatever it is we can work through it."

There was no response.

He turned his phone on and waited. There were a bunch of voicemails and text messages. He'd expected as much. He found Paige's number. She'd sent him a text every day he was gone telling him how much she loved and missed him.

Yet today, his stuff was sitting on the front porch. This made no sense. He scrolled all the way to the last text but found nothing unusual about it.

What was going on?

He flipped through the voicemail notifications. Nothing there either.

A Facebook notification popped up. That was weird. He rarely even looked at Facebook. In fact, he couldn't remember when'd been on there last.

He opened the app and stared at the picture that Debbie had taken of them eight years ago. Then he read the message and felt his stomach sinking. Of all the crappy things Debbie could do, this one took the cake. He had no idea she could be so vindictive. She never had been before.

Then again, he'd never turned her down in favor of another woman before. He pinched the bridge of his nose and then sent a quick text to Paige.

*I know what it looks like, but it's not true. Nothing happened between Debbie and me.*

He waited for just a moment before the three dots on the bottom of the screen showed that she was responding.

*I don't believe you. Go away.*

He swallowed. He had no idea how to convince her that it was true. Either she would believe him or not. But he wasn't getting anywhere standing on her front porch. He hadn't really slept in days, and that meant he'd make poor decisions like breaking open a window and not leaving until she believed him.

He grabbed the suitcase and dragged it down the driveway. He'd crash at Anna and Hayden's place and get Lukas to tell him how to convince Paige he was telling the truth.

He just hoped Lukas would believe him.

## CHAPTER 41

Paige woke with a start.
She'd had a nightmare again, but this one was different. She'd been standing in a room watching Blake and Debbie make out.

Why couldn't she be normal?

Instead, she had a dead husband who cheated on her, and it was her fault he was dead, and a boyfriend who's hung up on another woman.

She picked up her phone and glanced at the time. It was three-thirty in the morning. She'd missed a half-dozen texts from Blake and four calls, all with voicemails. She didn't want to see what they said.

Instead, she flicked on the TV and scrolled through Netflix. She went straight for the depressing dramas. She didn't want to laugh or fall in love, and adventure would be too intense right now.

Paige basically stayed in bed for three days. Her doorbell rang a few times, and she didn't answer her phone. She did send a text to Ida to let her know that she was fine, just not feeling well and that, no, she didn't want her to come over and bring her famous chicken noodle soup.

On day four, she glanced at the empty ice cream cartons and chip bags. Crumbs were all over her bed. And she smelled.

She crawled out of bed and turned the shower on to steaming hot. Then she stepped in and let the water run over her.

The tears came without warning, and within minutes she was curled in a ball bawling her eyes out. She missed Blake with every fiber of her being and his betrayal broke her. She sobbed until she couldn't cry anymore, letting the hot water wash the tears away. Then she stood and washed her hair.

When she stepped out of the shower, she felt like a new person. She still hurt from Blake's betrayal, but she felt better.

After she finished getting ready, she surveyed the mess in her bed. Her phone was buzzing somewhere in the middle, and she dug around until she found it.

Tess.

Without bothering to think too much, she answered it.

"You know. If you hadn't answered, Lukas was going to come out and force you to come home with him."

Paige sighed. "I know. I'm sorry. I just had to mope for a few days. I'm feeling better now."

"Lukas wants to talk to you and make sure you're doing okay."

Paige didn't really want to talk to him, but she didn't see that she had any choice. "Okay. Put him on."

"You really need to learn to answer your phone," Lukas snapped.

"Well, hello to you too."

"Paige, I've been extremely patient with you since Emery died, but today I'm going to tell you some things that might hurt."

"I've been hurt enough, Lukas. I don't need it from you too." After everything she went through with Blake, she didn't need Lukas to add to it.

"You made a mistake with Blake."

Paige's blood ran cold. "Who I date is my business. You don't get to lecture me on mistakes I've made."

"That's not what I meant. I meant that you should've given him the benefit of the doubt. He's staying with Hayden right now, but he's been over here every day asking for advice on how to get you back."

"What about Debbie?" Paige spat out. She hated even saying her name.

"She's an asshole. Nothing happened between her and Blake during their little work thing."

"Then why did she post on Facebook?"

"Did you not hear me? Because she's an asshole." Then his tone softened. "Because she wants Blake back, but he doesn't want her. He wants you."

Paige wanted to believe him, but there was too much evidence to the contrary. She saw the Facebook post. She wanted desperately to believe him, but she didn't want to be taken for a fool either.

"Yeah. I don't believe that."

"Then you're making a massive mistake. You know when I found out Blake and you had a thing going on, I worried mostly about you getting hurt. I never imagined you'd be the one to break his heart."

Paige had had enough. She hung up the phone and left it on her dresser.

She wasn't going to talk to anyone else today.

## CHAPTER 42

*B*lake rubbed his already red eyes and stared up at Lukas. He'd had the call on speakerphone, but Paige didn't know. It was good to hear her voice, but he'd hoped Lukas would've been able to convince her to talk to him.

He had no idea what else to do.

Tess sat next to him and rubbed his back. "Just give her some time."

"I don't want to give her time. Every day that I'm away from her, it physically hurts. Right here." He thumped his fist to his chest, which didn't help the ache residing there.

Lukas didn't say anything, and after a few minutes, Blake got up. "I'm going back to Hayden's."

He trudged out of the room and down the porch stairs. He paused at the end of the yard and sent another text to Paige.

*I love you so much. Please believe me. Nothing happened with Debbie. I can't stop thinking about you. Just let me* come home. *I'll spend the rest of the year making it up to you.*

It was pretty much the same text and voicemail he'd left her a hundred times already. But he didn't know what else to say. He couldn't live without her. She was just like Lukas, assuming the worst, though now Lukas was on his side. He hated that she thought so little of him.

That stupid post by Debbie. If she'd just take it down, maybe Paige would believe him. Blake started walking down the street and scrolled through his messages.

Debbie responded to the first three but refused to remove the post. Then she just stopped responding.

He punched the number next to her name and held the phone to his ear.

She answered after the first two rings. "Looks like you are finally over your rebound. Where are we meeting? The Keys are good. Though you do owe me a Hawaii trip."

"Take the post down," he growled.

She laughed, and he hated the sound. "Now why would I do that when we both know it's just a matter of time until it's true."

"Because it's not true, and it's ruining my relationship."

"Blake, if all it took to ruin your relationship was a misleading Facebook post, then you've got bigger problems than me. Why don't you admit to yourself that she's clearly not for you and meet me in Maui."

He hung up the phone. This was useless.

Her words stung though. Maybe he and Paige were kidding themselves. Maybe their relationship wasn't as strong as Blake thought.

Whatever it was, they could work through it.

He'd give her another week, and then he'd go back to town, stay with Ida and Phil, and do whatever it took to win her back.

# CHAPTER 43

"There's no way to know if he's lying or not." Paige stood on her deck, looking over the water. Blake had been gone a week now, and going back to her hermit ways had been so easy.

Stormy cursed on the other side of the phone. "I'm sorry you're going through this. Have you talked to him?"

"No. He's called me a bunch, and he sends me a text every day telling me that he loves and misses me. But I haven't responded or answered. Lukas did call me though to try to convince me to talk to him."

"Why?"

"Because he seems to think that Blake is telling the truth."

"Where is Blake now? Do you know?"

"Yeah, he's staying on Mackinac with other friends."

"And is Debbie there?"

"If she was, Lukas wouldn't be standing up for him."

In her mind, she knew this logically, but she still couldn't ignore what they had.

"So I've listened to your whole story now. Do you want my opinion?"

"Stormy, I always want your opinion."

"Okay, so the way I see it, everyone talks about Debbie being the love of his life, but he went on a work trip, and she was there. She dumped her hubby and probably wanted to get back together with him, but he's not with her right now, is he?"

"No."

"Everyone who knows him is telling you to trust him, and based on what I can see, I'm telling you the same thing. If something really had happened between them, he'd be with her, not moping at a friend's house. You need to let your guard down a little and just be happy with him."

"But I don't know if I trust him or not."

"Why? Because of Emery? They are not the same people, and you know it. Give him a chance to prove that. He sounds like a good guy who once upon a time had bad taste in women. Go, embrace what you have. Not many people get that."

Maybe Stormy was right. Paige had missed him terribly since he'd left. She said goodbye and looked at the phone.

One phone call and he'd be on his way back to her.

But she didn't want to call him. She wanted to see him. To look in his eyes and make sure he was telling the truth. Then she'd know for sure.

She slipped into the house and stared at the keys hanging on the rack by the door.

She hadn't driven since the accident, and she wasn't sure she was ready now, but she had to see him.

She plucked the keys off the rack and grabbed her purse. She opened the garage door to the small SUV that had taunted her the last few months. She slid into the driver's seat and waited.

Was she ready for this?

She tapped the ON button and felt the engine start up. Then she put her hands on the wheel.

She could do this.

## CHAPTER 44

Blake dragged himself out of bed. He didn't want to get up, but the last time he slept past ten, Anna sent little Mason in to wake him up. She didn't let him mope around.

Blake didn't know how to win Paige back. He'd been to Lukas's house every day this week, but Lukas didn't know what to do either.

At least he believed him.

The problem was that Paige didn't. She'd cut him off completely.

No. He refused to believe it was over.

She was hurt and upset, but Blake would find a way to get back into her good graces.

He took a quick shower and then jogged down the stairs. He found a note on the counter. *Gone into town, will be back this afternoon. There is a bagel in the fridge for you. Don't go back to bed. Lukas will be over at noon to take you out.*

He rolled his eyes. He loved his friends, but sometimes they were a little much. Though, he had to admit to himself that if the tables were turned, he'd do the same thing. He glanced at the clock. It was eleven forty-five. Lukas would be here soon.

Instead of eating the bagel, he opted for a banana and went in search of his shoes. He had no idea what Lukas had planned for him, but he hoped it would be something that would take his mind off everything. And include food.

The doorbell rang. Damn, he was early.

He jerked the front door open. "Anna said I had…"

Standing on the front porch was not Lukas at all. It was Paige.

"What are you doing here?" His first instinct was to reach out and pull her in for a hug, but he withheld because he didn't want to drive her away.

"I need to talk to you." She wrung her hands and wouldn't look him in the eyes.

He reached for her. He couldn't help himself.

She backed away, and he let out a breath. "How did you get here?"

"I drove and then took the ferry."

"You drove?" He wondered what possessed her to finally cross that hurdle. He was so proud of her, but he was still confused.

"Yes. Did you sleep with her?"

"What?"

"Debbie, did you sleep with her?" She finally met his eyes and he found determination behind hers.

"No." He said it with conviction. He needed Paige to understand that absolutely nothing at all happened. "I wasn't even tempted, if you want the truth."

She searched his eyes. "Did you kiss her?"

"No."

"Do you love her?"

He shook his head. "I don't. I thought I did, and then I met you. I love you more than life itself."

She nodded. "Okay, then. I believe you."

"You believe me?" That seemed easier than it should've been, but he wasn't going to turn it down.

"Yes."

"So can I kiss you now?" He closed the distance between them, wanting to believe that she meant it and that their fight was over.

"Yeah, you can."

He grinned and brought his lips to hers. She wound her arms around his neck and deepened the kiss. After a good long kiss, one in which he debated bringing her back up to his room, he pulled away.

"I'm so sorry you had to go through that." He didn't want to cause her pain like that ever again.

She shrugged and her face turned serious. "I'm glad you didn't sleep with her and that you love me. I've missed you."

"You too. I don't ever want to be away from you again."

"Me neither. You're stuck with me now, because even though I managed to drive all the way over here, I like it better when you drive."

He grinned. "Okay. Under one condition."

"What's that?"

"Marry me."

She glared at him. "I thought we'd been over this. I'm not answering until there is a ring and big to-do."

"A big to-do, huh?"

"Yes."

He grinned. "Just remember that you asked for it."

He kissed her again, his mind already planning the best proposal ever.

# EPILOGUE

Grayson stood on the beach with David and Seth, surrounded by ten dogs.

"You know," Seth said, "we got handed the short end of the stick."

"Because we're the only single guys left?" Grayson asked.

David crouched down and scratched Tria behind her ears. "Nah, we got the best job. All we have to do is let the dogs go."

"Speak for yourself," Grayson grumbled. He'd been tasked with holding the balloons, which wasn't easy because of the wind.

Dani, Grayson's best friend in the whole world, jogged up to them. "It's almost time." She held up the bag in her hand, her eyes glittering.

"We should probably get the rings attached," David said.

Grayson glanced down at the ring on Dani's finger. The one that wasn't from him, and his chest tightened.

"Who proposes with ten rings?" Dani asked, securing a ring on Dio's collar.

"Paige teased Blake that she wanted big to-do, so he went over the top on everything. She's been on a scavenger hunt all day hunting for clues as to where she's supposed to go. It's taken all of us and the wives to pull this off."

Dani glanced at her own half-carat diamond. "Jeremy didn't have quite that much fun with my proposal."

"How did he propose?" Seth asked, trying to catch Nona, who thought this was a game.

Dani just shrugged and took a couple of balloons from Grayson. "He just handed me the ring one night at dinner and proposed."

Grayson didn't correct her. She'd called him in tears that night because instead of a proposal, he basically left the ring on the counter and Paige found it. She took it out into the living room where Jeremy had been playing video games and asked him about it.

He didn't even pause the game. He just said, "You said we were done if we didn't get married. So, there's your ring. We can head down to the justice of the peace tomorrow."

She didn't put the ring on for three days, and he had the audacity to ask her why she wasn't wearing it. She put it on eventually but demanded a real wedding, since if Jeremy knew anything about Dani he'd have known that she'd been planning her wedding day since she was five.

Hayden jogged up to them. "It's time."

"Oh crap. We're not ready." Grayson handed Hayden three of the balloons, and they quickly went about adhering them to what he hoped was the right dog. The balloons spelled out "Marry me?" with a heart balloon on the first and last dog.

Hayden led the way with Grayson, David, and Seth, trying to make sure the dogs stayed in a line. They were mostly successful.

On the beach, Grayson spotted Blake and Paige. Blake had one arm around Paige, and he pointed to the sky with the other. Grayson glanced up and saw a skywriter also popping the question.

Grayson rolled his eyes but couldn't help his smile.

"This is the most romantic thing in the entire world," Dani said, her face glowing.

"That it is. I think it's a little much though."

"I don't," Dani said.

"Of course you don't. Your wedding is going to be the most over-the-top wedding of the century."

She bumped him with her hip. "It is not. It's perfect."

"Whatever you say." Then he grinned at her. "I have planned the most epic bachelorette party on the planet though."

She pointed at Seth, who walked about three feet in front of them. "Unless it involves that man as a stripper, it won't be all that epic."

Seth turned and grinned. "I'm definitely available."

"Absolutely not. I promised her a bachelorette party, not an affair the night before her wedding." Not that Dani would cheat on Jeremy, but he wouldn't put it past Seth to try.

Dani always flirted with Seth from the day they met. Though truth be told, he'd rather see her with Seth than Jeremy. That guy was the biggest prick on the planet. But Dani swore she loved him, and that he was different when they were alone.

Grayson didn't buy it.

They got the dogs to surround Blake and Paige, and all stepped back a little, except Jamie, who was busy taking pictures. Blake got down on one knee and seconds later, Paige squealed out a yes.

Dani wove her arm around Grayson's back and rested her head on his shoulder. "Definitely the most romantic thing ever."

Grayson just nodded.

Dani deserved that as well.

But as much as he wanted to, he couldn't be the guy to give it to her.

Because she was in love with someone else.

*To Be Continued in Grayson...*

Dear Reader,

So funny story. When I first imagined Blake's book, I'd actually had him getting back together with Debbie, but as I wrote more and more of the Michigan Millionaires books it became clear that he and Debbie were not meant to be. I do hope you enjoyed his and Paige's story.

And are you ready for Grayson? This is another that changed dramatically for me. Originally David was supposed to come next, but one day I was driving down the road and listening to sappy country music and suddenly a whole new story popped into my head and Grayson was the star. Pre-order this friends to lovers book now: *Voyages and Vows.*

As always if you loved the book or even if you didn't, please leave a review.

Thanks for being a fan,

Xoxo

Kim

**P.S. Stay in touch!P.S. Stay in touch through my Kimberly Loth pen name!**

1) I'm starting a text subscription service! If you sign up to get texts, you'll get:
- **6 FREE eBOOKS (all my 1st in series)!**
- **Exclusive alerts for all my sales, freebies & releases (you'll always be the first to know)!**

**\*\*To join, text BOOKS to (877) 949-4667.**
See below for text disclaimers, including instructions for international fans.

2) We're going to spend the rest of the year having one big party to celebrate my upcoming releases. Come join us: **facebook.com/groups/KimberlyLothReleaseParty**

**Want More from Kimmy Loth?**

*Read about all the fraternity brothers in the Michigan Millionaires series*

Text Service disclaimers:

*excluding boxed sets
**You agree to receive automated promotional messages. This agreement isn't a condition of any purchase. Terms and Privacy Policy can be found at kimberlyloth.com/privacy. You may receive multiple messages month. Reply STOP to end or HELP for help.

This service is available for continental U.S. fans only, however international fans can join a NL group with the same promotions. For details email kimberlylothteam@gmail.com

ALSO BY KIMMY LOTH

**Michigan Millionaires (Sweet Romance Series)**

Snowfall and Secrets

Folly and Forever

Monkeys and Mayhem

**Michigan Millionaires Box Set Books 1-3**

Roadtrips and Romance

Christmas and Commitment

Pyramids and Promises

**Michigan Millionaires Box Set Books 4-6**

Lakesides and Longing

# ABOUT THE AUTHOR

Kimmy Loth has lived all over the world. From the isolated woods of the Ozarks to exotic city of Cairo. She currently lives on the beautiful Sugar Creek in southern Missouri with her sweet little dog, Maisy.

She's been writing for twelve years and also writes under the pen name Kimberly Loth. In her free time she volunteers at church, reads, and travels as often as possible.

She loves talking to school groups and book clubs. For more information about having her come speak at your school or event contact her at kimberlyloth@gmail.com.

Printed in Great Britain
by Amazon

Printed in Great Britain
by Amazon

36936036R00118